D0127004

For Terry and Norm, with love

Prologue

Summer Of The Year 2000

'It's haunted,' says Auburn, poking Willow so hard in her skinny ribcage that she almost falls over. She rights herself by clinging on to her brother, Angel, who is almost as skinny as her, and trying to look completely unaffected by the whole adventure.

As part of his attempt at bravado, he pushes Willow away with both hands. She's the youngest of the siblings by several years – always smaller, always quieter, always the butt of the jokes, always on the receiving end of the pranks. Always determined to prove that she's not the weakest link, and usually getting herself into trouble along the way.

'No it's not,' says Willow, staggering a few steps along the corridor and bumping into the wood-panelled wall. It's an old building, this, all dark wallpaper and high ceilings and ornate plasterwork. It's big, and filled with labyrinth-like corridors full of mystery. It's also been, for this one summer, their unofficial – and slightly terrifying – playground.

'It's *not!*' she repeats, glaring at Auburn in defiance. 'You can't have only one room haunted in a whole massive house. That doesn't make sense!'

'Course it does,' says Auburn, looking to her big brother for back-up, red hair flashing in the dim lighting. Van is fifteen, and the oldest of the gang. He's already six foot tall and has the musculature of a runner bean to go with his unfashionable Nirvana T-shirt and shoulder-length grease-bomb hair. He thinks he's really cool, which doesn't quite make up for the fact that everyone else thinks he's a complete dork.

Willow gazes up at him from her significantly shorter eight-year-old's height, frowning. She's worshipped her big brother for a long time, but is starting to suspect that he might actually be evil. He definitely smells evil. She eyes the stains on his T-shirt, knowing that in a few years' time, as soon as she's big enough, she'll be expected to wear it. Hand-me-downs are a way of life for the Longville family.

All three of the younger siblings stare at Van, waiting for his pronouncement. Auburn looks fierce; Angel is biting his chubby lip and trembling, and Willow has her arms crossed defiantly over her passed-down-several-times Barney the Purple Dinosaur T-shirt.

'It could be . . .' he says, creeping towards the door at the end of the corridor, '. . . that the evil spirit only resides in this particular room. Maybe something terrible happened there.'

'Like what?' asks Willow, trying to sound tough but

wishing she could just run away and find her mum. She knows she can't, though – Auburn would never let her live it down. Besides, her mum is leading some kind of meditation workshop out in the garden, and she'll kill her if she interrupts it. Well, not kill her exactly – something a bit more zen then that, but it wouldn't be good.

'Like,' says Auburn, whispering into her ear, 'someone died in there. Maybe they hung themselves from the rafters. Or maybe they were bricked up in the wall and left to starve to death. Or maybe it was a little crippled boy whose parents were ashamed of him and kept him in there his whole life, until he wasted away.'

Angel looks on the verge of tears now, his blonde curls bobbling around his full cheeks. Van is nodding wisely, as though every word Auburn has just said makes perfect sense to his almost-adult mind.

'That's . . . crap!' replies Willow, flushing slightly as she uses what she knows is a naughty word. Not sent-to-bed naughty, like the ones Van uses that start with F, but still naughty. Somehow, though, using it gives her the strength to do what she does next.

'Prove it, then,' taunts Auburn, pointing at the door. 'Go and open it and see what's inside. If you dare.'

The door in question, just minutes ago, looked completely ordinary, but now – after her 14-year-old sister has finished creating a whole myth around it – looks utterly horrifying. Dark wood, brass handle, empty keyhole. Practically the gates to hell.

It's just a door, Willow tells herself, glaring at Auburn with the sort of hatred that only a younger sister can feel for someone she loves.

It's just a door, to a room, that isn't haunted. Because ghosts don't exist, and even if they did, they might be friendly, like Casper.

She draws in a ragged breath, and tucks her straggly brown hair behind her ears. More than anything right now, she wishes they hadn't started this game. They know most of the kids who live here, in this place – a place where kids with no mum or dad come to live. They know their names, and their stories, and they play with them while their own mum is working, doing art classes or yoga lessons or helping them with their reading.

They know most of them – but they don't know who lives in that room. The door has never been open, the child who lives in there has never been seen, and the only evidence they have of his existence is the occasional shadowy glimpse through the window outside.

That's what started it all – this debate about whether he was real, or a ghost. It was fun to start off with – but now? Now it's very scary indeed. Willow doesn't really want to open the door. She doesn't want to see the spirit of someone hanging from the rafters with their purple tongue bulging out, or encounter a half-starved child who's sure to be a bit angry with the world.

But she wants Auburn to see her weakness even less. Auburn is always mean to her, and always manages to hide it from their mum, which makes Willow look like she's always moaning about nothing. If she backs out now, she'll never let her forget it. Right on cue, she hears her big sister start making chicken noises behind her, and within seconds, the boys have joined in, flapping their arms like wings and clucking away in a poultry-inspired chorus.

Willow wipes her face with Barney – she's sweating now, even though the dark hallway is cool – and takes a couple of tenuous steps forward. Ignoring the clucks, she finds her stride, and treads across the threadbare carpet towards the end of the corridor. Towards the door, and either glory, or potential death – she's not quite sure.

She pauses outside, and waits for a moment, her fingers resting on the handle. She glances behind her, and sees their faces; Van, looking amused, Angel, frowning, and Auburn staring at her like she just *knows* she's going to break.

That spurs her on, and Willow, with trembling hands, finally turns the handle, and pushes open the door. It creaks, and stiffens, and finally – finally – swings back.

She freezes, a tiny, scared figure in a too-big Barney T-shirt, eyes wide with terror as she looks inside.

The room is dark, the curtains drawn but not quite meeting in the middle – the only light coming in through the window is casting pale stripes over a cluttered desk. A desk that is scattered with coils and springs and cannibalised pieces of machinery, which her young mind immediately associates with the project on medieval torture devices that Angel did the year before.

Sitting in front of the desk, turning to face her, is a boy. Maybe a ghost boy, maybe a real one. She really can't tell in the dimness. He's older than her, with pale skin and dark hair, and eyes that are huge and brown and shocked over pronounced cheekbones. He has a screwdriver in his hand, and his gaze is almost as fearful as hers as he stares at her, blinking as the sudden light from the corridor floods in, drenching him in sinister shadow.

Even if he's not a ghost, he looks haunted – and this is enough to send Willow over the edge.

She screams, loud and shrill, and slams the door shut again. She collapses on the floor in a shaking heap, and looks up at her brothers and sister, crowding around her.

They're shaking too, she notices. With laughter. Auburn is pointing at her, and holding her sides, and Van seems to actually have tears running down his face. Angel, as ever, is copying them.

She climbs up onto unsteady legs, and runs away, humiliated and scared, knocking them viciously out of the way as she flees. She hates them right now – all of them.

Her little legs barrel her down the wooden staircase, and if the big door to the house hadn't already been open, she might have crashed through it like a cartoon character, leaving a Willow-shaped hole in the oak.

She runs off down the gravel-topped path at the side of the house, and away to the wood, and the secret pond she likes. She collapses onto a moss-covered log, and kicks her trainer-clad feet at the shale and sticks and old leaves that have collected on the floor like a collage, catching her breath.

Being alone calms her down, and she knows she'll be all right. He wasn't really a ghost, after all. Ghosts don't use screwdrivers and look scared when little girls burst into their rooms, do they?

She spends the rest of the morning playing quietly alone by the pond, still not quite ready to re-engage with the feral pack that is her family. Still, in her childlike way, haunted by that pale face and those big, dark eyes.

Chapter 1

The Present Day

My name is Willow Longville. I am twenty-six years old. I live in a village called Budbury, with my mum Lynnie. I work as a waitress at the Comfort Food Café, and I run my own cleaning business called Will-o'-the-Wash. I have a dog called Bella Swan, and I love my life. In the last twenty-four hours, the following things have happened . . .

1. My friend Cherie convinced us she was pregnant and expecting twins. This came as a surprise as Cherie is seventy-four. She told us she'd been to a fertility clinic in Montenegro and we believed her for about five minutes.
2. Bella Swan ate a frog.
3. The Comfort Food Café officially opened a bookshop. We celebrated with cakes decorated with pictures of famous literary characters like Oliver Twist, Tess of the D'Urbervilles, Mr Darcy and the scary clown from *It*. That last one was my idea, and it was pretty creepy eating Pennywise's face.

4. My mother attacked me with a frying pan when she thought I'd broken into the house.
5. I slept for maybe three minutes after that, as she'd also called the police.
6. I woke up to sunshine and it made me happy. Then I ate leftover Harry Potter cake from the café for breakfast, which made me even happier.
7. I came back to the House on the Hill, and even though it's still scary, it seems a lot smaller now I'm not a kid. Technically at least.
8. I went for a walk to the pond first, and saw a naked man dappled in sunlight in the water, and his skin was shining like diamonds – I am now a bit concerned that I have conjured up a real life Edward Cullen.

I pause in my list making, and decide to stop. There's really no way to top seeing an imaginary Edward Cullen in a pond, is there?

Instead, I sit, still and quiet, perched on the edge of the dried-up fountain, and enjoy the moment.

It's the first truly warm day of spring, and Mother Nature has come out to celebrate. In fact, she's downed a bottle of vodka and is having a full-on rave – the woods are swathed in new greenery, the grass is lush and thick, and carpets of bluebells are springing up in the clearings, waving their hands in the air like they just don't care.

It's all shockingly beautiful, and my spirits are flying so

high they could almost touch the sun. You know, if they had fingers.

Today, I tell myself, is going to be a Good Day. It started off bad, then veered off into strange, and now it's my job to make the rest of it good.

This isn't quite as easy as it sounds, with the House on the Hill looming behind me in all its hideous glory.

I can't shake the feeling that it looks like something from a horror film. One of those horror films where the parents think it's a good idea to give their kid the creepiest-looking doll in the world, and you spend most of it yelling: 'Just get out! Go and stay in a bloody Travelodge for God's sake!'

Technically, this brick-built extra from Amityville is called Briarwood – but to all us locals, it's also the House on the Hill. There are some devilishly complicated reasons for that nickname; A, it's a house, and B, it's on a hill. Yeah, I know – bet that foxed you. Nothing if not sharp, us country bumpkins.

Even the hill is pretty scary – a clutch-churning demon where you have to rev up the incline in first gear, hoping you don't roll all the way back down again if you do something reckless like sneeze, or sing along to Katy Perry's 'Roar' a bit too enthusiastically.

I haven't been here for ages – not since I was a kid, in fact. That, both in years and experience, feels like several lifetimes ago. It's getting on for twenty years now, which is a bit freaky. I gaze back at the building, and I suspect my face is looking a bit like my face usually looks when I'm scooping up dog poo and my finger pokes through the bag.

The red brick facade has scaffolding around it, but if there are any workmen, they're invisible. The big, blue-painted wooden door is still standing, although it needs some TLC. The old windows still have their Gothic stone twirls around the frames, and the roof still looks like it needs a few gargoyles to complete its American Horror Story vibe. The fountain I'm sitting on has a stone-carved cherub in the middle, and is clogged with weeds and algae.

The gardens and shrubberies are overgrown and tangled, but someone seems to have been making some headway. Whoever it was must have had a machete, and possibly an army of Oompa Loompas to help him. I automatically start singing the Oompa Loompa song at that point, which isn't quite as melodic as the background sounds of birdsong and the breeze ruffling the leaves of the oak trees.

It's very strange to be back here, and it takes a lot to qualify as strange in my world. If I close my eyes, turn my face up to the sun, and stop singing the Ooompa Loompa song, I can almost travel back in time. I can hear the sound of my brothers and sister laughing; their footsteps scudding across the gravel; my mother chanting something insanely silly that she tries to convince people is a sign of deep spiritual awakening while a bunch of teenagers try to stifle their giggles.

That particular memory – the one of my much younger

mum – makes me feel a tinge of sadness, so I try and put it away in a box and jump on its head. I'm wearing Doc Martens mentally as well as physically, so I give it a good old stomp to make sure it stays down.

It's been a mad twenty-four hours, and getting no less mad now I'm here, after that brief and possibly hallucinogenic detour to the pond in the woods first. I know I'm tired, even if I don't actually feel it – I've trained myself out of noticing fatigue in the last few years, but it still lurks inside me, like a jack-in-the-box waiting to spring up and catch me. And when I'm tired, my thought processes tend to trip over themselves, impossible to follow.

Yep. It's been a weird start to the day – but now I have to make it better. Only I can do that, and I need to focus on the sunshine and the birdsong instead of taking a trip on a memory train that will deposit me in a lonely station at the end of the line.

I re-read the list, and think it's a fairly good summary of my day. I also seem to have accidentally created my very own psychedelic acid trip without the need for any pharmaceuticals at all: the neon pink notepad and bright green gel pen are resting on my knees, and I'm wearing leggings with pictures of yellow Minions on them. Funky.

I stretch my arms, and glory in the feel of the sun on my skin. It's like God has reached down to stroke my face – and He's wearing really warm oven gloves.

It's been a long, nasty winter, and I feel that sense of absolute amazement I get every year when the spring arrives. It's odd, because it does happen every single year – but each time, I'm taken aback by it. Our quiet corner of Dorset has had a lot of snow over the cold months, and I've been used to wearing long johns and seventeen pairs of gloves every day. Now, much to my surprise, it's warm again . . . who'd have thunk it?

'What do you reckon, Bella?' I say, to the dog sleeping at my feet. 'Time to get to work?'

Bella doesn't answer. Mainly because she's a ten-year-old Border Terrier, and not exactly the chatty type. She doesn't even bark, never mind talk.

She does get up though, making direct eye contact with me while she squats down and has a wee, as though that's her way of replying.

'Yeah. Well, I'm glad you agree,' I say, as I walk towards my van to get my cleaning supplies.

My van is small and white and has a rainbow painted on the side. My mum painted the rainbow, and we're both very proud of it. There's a dream catcher hanging in the window, and Mum decorated the back with some ancient, yellowing stickers she found in a drawer – telling people to Ban the Bomb, Save the Whales and Hug a Tree. Sound advice, as long as you don't get them confused and end up hugging a bomb, or banning the poor whales.

Whenever I drive it, it kind of looks like I should be giving hitch-hikers a lift to a festival in 1976, or protesting at Greenham Common, or going on tour with Led Zeppelin. It's actually full of cleaning products, some of which I have to hide from my mother because they contain chemicals stronger than baking soda. My mother has Alzheimer's, and often doesn't know who I am – but she can spot a planet-killing detergent at 300 yards.

Bella, tired from her toilet efforts, lies on the grass. She stares with very little interest at a small flight of swallows who are also celebrating the unexpected return of spring, swirling and diving around the fountain. She lets out one very ladylike fart, then curls up into a furry ball. I remain unconvinced that any part of her genetic make-up is descended from a wolf.

I put my notepad down on the front seat, and realise I need to start a new one soon. I never expected to enjoy it so much, but I do. I start every entry with the same words – name, rank and serial number – before making my 'What's Happened to Willow Today' list.

It's a bit long-winded, but it's become a habit – and as habits go, it's not as bad as, say, crack cocaine or eating your own bogies in public (in private is a different matter – we've all done it).

I started the note-keeping when Mum's case worker recommended she do something called Life Story Work. As by that stage my mum's life story seemed to have stopped – in her mind at least – at about 1999, it seemed like a good idea.

It's a way of helping her stay in touch with her memories and regain an element of control – reminding herself of who she was and who she is, I suppose. Sometimes I catch her reading it quietly, glancing up at me every now and then, and I know she's trying to re-make the connections between her little girl and the grown-up woman standing before her.

Yes, it's sad – but it's happy too, in its own way. Celebratory. And she's really good at it. She's always been one of those craftsy people, my mum, and her book is a beautiful patchwork collage of photos and postcards and old ticket stubs and even those little plastic bracelets they put on babies in hospital. It's part life story, part diary, part practical – amid the reminiscences and memories, she'll add in little reminders, like her address, and my phone number, and the name of the dog. We've had a series of Border Terriers, and she sometimes gets them confused.

At first, I started up my own notepad just to keep her company and make it all feel a bit less weird. But I've got into it – and who knows? Maybe one day I'll need it myself. Scary dairy. For the time being, it's a bit of free therapy at least.

I usually make lists in it, as I don't have a lot of time on my own to sit and indulge in stream of consciousness rants. Lists keep it simple and usually make me laugh when I read them back. I once wrote the words 'sausage rolls are brilliant'. On ten separate lines. I guess I'd really enjoyed a sausage roll that day.

Today, though . . . well, today, I had lots to report, didn't I? Especially about the imaginary Edward Cullen, who may or may not be real, and may or may not be the new owner of Briarwood.

There has been much talk in the village about this new owner. About who it might be, and when he or she might get here, and whether they'll be part of the gang or just play lord of the manor. About why they wanted to buy the place at all, given the state of it. We've spent literally hours debating it in the café. What can I say? Not much happens round here.

Frank, Cherie's husband, reckons it's some foreign investor who's going to tart it up as a posh corporate retreat for stressed executives. Frank is a farmer, but he has a vivid imagination. Edie May, who is almost ninety-two and has an even better imagination, reckons it's been bought by Tom Cruise as a holiday home – but she's not been quite right since her niece bought her a *Mission: Impossible* box set. Laura, who manages the café and is a bit of a soppy romantic, is convinced that it's a young couple looking for a dream home to raise a family in.

I'm here at Briarwood because I'm being paid to clean the place, by an estate agent in Bristol. My mum is safe and snug with Cherie at the café, and they'll all be waiting for me to get back – desperate for me to spill the beans and fill them in on what I've seen.

The problem is, as things stand, I'm going to have to tell them all that the House on the Hill has, in fact, been bought by an eternally teenaged vegetarian vampire. That should raise a few eyebrows.

Chapter 2

Inside, the house isn't quite as daunting as I remembered. It's been empty since Mr and Mrs Featherbottom – yes, that's their real name – retired, over a decade ago.

They'd moved to a flat in Lyme Regis, after spending years running Briarwood as some kind of private children's home. That sounds terrifying in itself, but all my memories of the couple are really nice. Mrs F was round and often covered in flour; Mr F always seemed to have a fishing rod in his hand. In fact, I think perhaps I'm getting confused, and imagining them both as garden gnomes come to life.

From what I can recall, and from what the older residents of Budbury like Frank and Edie have said, it was quite a happy place – considering the circumstances of most of the kids. Some of them were orphans, which sounds pretty Dickensian; others were placed there because their parents just couldn't be their mum and dad for some reason, like illness or work. It was part home, part boarding school.

Some of the children arrived in various states of distress

– and pulling up in front of a building that looks like it might be patrolled by Dementors at night probably didn't help.

That's one of the reasons my mum used to come here. To help the kids. She was always a little on the feral side, my mum – never had what you'd call a proper job in her life. My three older siblings – Van, Angel and Auburn – spent the first years of their lives on a hippy artists' commune in Cornwall, until I came along. Different dad, a few years later – which at least partly explains why I've always been the odd one out.

They all moved to Budbury while Mum was pregnant with me, and she picked up bits of work here and there – enough to keep us in gender-neutral clothes that could always be passed down, as well as funding our hummus and pitta bread habit. I suppose she was ahead of her time in a lot of ways – trying to get us to eat organic, never taking us to the doctor unless a leg was about to drop off, giving us weird names before Gwyneth Paltrow ever thought of it.

Here at Briarwood, she did a variety of things – yoga classes, meditation, arts and crafts sessions, creative writing workshops. She was just Mum to us, but I think to a lot of the kids she must have seemed like an insanely exotic creature, all wild curly hair and tie-dye clothes, smelling of incense and Patchouli oil.

As I wander the corridors of the building, I can still see the signs of all that life – all those young people, living here together, with Mr and Mrs F trying to make it as nice for them as they could. There are still old noticeboards on the walls downstairs, the tattered remains of tacked-up paper dangling from rusted drawing pins. I know I need to clear them off, but it feels a bit like I'm somehow defiling a sacred place. Vandalising a museum, maybe.

I pull one down, and part of the paper disintegrates in my hand. I can still see what it was about, though: Mr F taking part in a sponsored Fish-a-Thon to raise money for Save the Children. I smile, and place the sheet inside two pages of my notepad. I don't quite have the heart to throw it into a bin bag, which might explain why my bedroom is cluttered enough to qualify me for one of those reality TV shows about hoarders.

I continue my investigations, leaving the front door propped open with a brick – there is electricity in here, I've found, but a lot of the lightbulbs are blown, and others are flickering as I go. I'm already slightly jumpy, and the sizzling sounds of the overhead lamps and the on-again-off-again light quality isn't helping. Luckily, I have my fearless guard dog with me – Bella has her nose to the ground, and is dashing around in strange looping circles that only make sense to her. She's making a snuffling sound like a seal as she goes, which is reassuring in an otherwise silent building.

I work my way towards what I remember was the office, and Mr and Mrs F's living quarters, and again find something of a time capsule. Most of the furniture is gone, but there are a few odds and ends: a pile of mouldy paperbacks; empty filing cabinets, open and gaping; the desiccated remains of a potted plant that may or may not have been an African violet in a previous life. The bay window is grimy, but sunshine is pouring in and dappling the whole room with dancing dust motes.

I try and shake off the impending sense of melancholy, and start thinking professionally instead. I know from the estate agent that the upper floors have been completely cleared. So, I tell the logical part of my brain – this is a very small part, with super-selective hearing – that's where I should start.

I'm booked for a few days, and there'll be plenty of time to get around to the lower floors later. It'll be easier once they're empty – apart from anything else, it'll stop me gazing at everything as though I have some weird telepathic power that allows me to talk to dead houseplants.

Bella is sniffing furiously at the paperbacks, and I know what that might mean.

'Nope,' I say firmly, reaching down to distract her with a tickle behind the ears. 'It might smell like it, but this is not the outside. So no puddles, okay?'

She gives me a look from beneath her grey, whiskery eyebrows, and trots off back into the corridor. I swear, she understands every word.

I retrieve my cleaning supplies – the usual exciting smorgasbord of cloths, chemicals and bin bags– and climb the wooden staircase up to the top floor. This will mainly be a reconnaissance mission – I'm guessing I'll have to come back with the heavy-duty floor cleaning gear later, and possibly rope in some of the strapping menfolk of the village to help me lug it up the stairs. Luckily we are insanely blessed with strapping menfolk in Budbury. It seems to be located on some kind of mystical ley line that pulls them in.

As I climb, I notice the thick layer of dust that's built up on the curving banister. This always used to be polished so well you could see your distorted face reflected in it – it was kept that way by a combination of Mrs F, Mr Sheen, and the bottoms of boisterous young kids sliding down it.

Briarwood was always bustling – there was always noise, and music, and activity, and the rich smells of cooking and communal living. Now, it's so sad and quiet and musty – and I realise I'm thrilled that someone has bought it. I hope Tom Cruise takes care of the place and doesn't turn it into a Scientologist bunker.

When I reach the top floor, it is much smaller in reality than in my recollections. In the same way that Mars Bars seemed much bigger back then, Briarwood also loomed large. I think I'd imagined it was an enormous mansion, filled with secret compartments and haunted stairwells. It certainly felt like it back then, especially compared to the crowded three-bedroomed cottage that we all lived in.

Now that it's shrunk – or I've grown – I see that there are probably no more than twenty rooms, laid out over three floors. It looks a bit like a smaller version of Professor Xavier's School for Gifted Youngsters, sadly minus Wolverine in his slinky vest top. I'm sure there's a cellar as well, but there's about as much chance of me going down there alone as there is of me completing a PhD in astrophysics.

I can see the marks where the carpet used to be, the floorboards around it more faded and dusty. The walls are bare, and each room I poke my head into is empty. The rooms vary in size, but are all decorated the same way – in blue wallpaper dotted with now-yellowing footballs, with threadbare blue carpet. I remember there were girls here as well. They probably all stayed on the floor below, in rooms with fairy princess wallpaper and pink carpet.

I'm guessing the new owner will sort all of this out. It's not my job to check the damp-proofing, or redecorate – it's my job to give it a once-over with the Will-o'-the-Wash magic touch. I'm assuming there will be some hefty reno- vations eventually, but making it less disgusting will be a start. My contribution to bringing this place back to life.

I decide to start with the windows – getting them clean will make the whole experience a lot more pleasant for everyone. By which I mean for me. The dirt and grime all over them is making the building feel even more neglected. It's a beautiful day outside, and I need to let some of that sunshine in.

I work my way through almost all of the rooms, opening the windows as I clean each one. Some need a bit of welly – they're crusted closed by old paint or grot, and I become intimate friends with several weirdly shaped lumps of moss as I go.

I gaze outside as I work, hoping for a glimpse of the man I saw in the pond earlier. He didn't see me – I edged away as quietly as I could when I realised there was someone there. Nobody wants to be caught out having a personal moment in a pond, do they? And, as I can't see any car parked nearby, it's still entirely possible that I imagined it.

I mean, I don't think I did. I'm not usually quite that out there. But I am very tired, I have had a hard couple of days, and I can't rule it out. Or, of course, he might just be someone who likes the pond and walks up here in the grounds of Briarwood – I'd noticed bits of litter, as well as old cider bottles and cigarette stubs, which is usually a sign of colonisation by the common or garden teenager.

He didn't look like a teenager – he was definitely grown-man shaped in all the right ways – but he could have been a walker. We get loads of walkers. Budbury is on the Jurassic Coast, and part of a network of clifftop paths that criss-cross the whole area. The Comfort Food Café is often visited by the kinds of people who wear high-vis singlets over their anoraks and use spiky poles to walk with. Maybe he was just one of those.

I try and put it to the back of my mind, and concentrate on the job. Bella has found a corner she likes the smell of, and is snoring away as I work. As I keep cleaning, the scent of lemons starts to gradually overpower the scent of neglect.

Each room has its own sink – they're filthy, and will probably be next on the list – but the plumbing is still functional, even if it is creaky, which means I can fill and refill my bowls to my heart's content.

It's mind-numbing work, and in all honesty that's one of the reasons I like it. It stops my brain from wandering, and there's also a very tangible outcome. You clean something, it ends up clean. It's not like so many other things in life where you put in megatons of effort and nothing seems to change as a result.

I'm hitting my stride, and building myself up to tackling the last room on the corridor, wishing I'd brought my radio or some speakers with me. I could put in my earphones, but hey – I've seen horror films. I know what happens to young women, alone in an old deserted house, when they don't pay attention. The only thing you can do that's worse than put earphones in is snog someone – the bogeyman will definitely get you if you do that. Stabbed to death in your bra and knickers, end of story.

I'm not about to snog anybody, but I do wish I had the music. Maybe a bit of Meatloaf, or the collected works of Neil Diamond – something with a big chorus to sing along to.

I'd like the distraction, as I'm now standing outside that last room. The one I've not even been into yet. Staring it down, as though I need to show it who's boss.

Not that it's any different than the others, I'm sure – it's just that we have a bit of history, me and that room. The last summer I spent any significant amount of time here, my darling siblings persuaded me it was haunted, and dared me to go in and find out.

I still remember vividly how scared I was. Even though it seems silly now, like most dramas from your childhood do in hindsight, I'm a wee bit hesitant as I walk towards it, bin bag in one hand, spray gun in the other. You know, just in case I need to spray cleaning fluid in a demon's eyes or anything.

I haven't seen my siblings for varying amounts of years. They've scattered like sheep, landing in different places doing different things. It's only me who's still here, in Budbury – with our mum. I don't blame them; they're older than me, and moved away and built their lives long before she started to show signs of her illness. I don't blame them – but I do miss them.

Even though, I think, as I pause outside the Room of Horrors, they were complete bastards that day – building up the terror, forcing me to go through with it, then laughing their arses off when I was so scared. It was the end for me and Briarwood – Mum kept on working here on and off, but I always made sure I had something else to do, even if it was tagging along with my evil big sister Auburn. Vicious as she could be, she wasn't as scary as that room.

Over the years, though, I've thought of it occasionally – the way that kids can be so casually cruel to each other and not give it a second thought.

And, of course, the way I ran away, frightened out of my wits – I didn't even talk to the poor boy in the room, who was just as scared. Who wouldn't be? Some strange, feral child crashes into your space uninvited, screams at the top of her voice, and legs it without a word of explanation?

I think I scarred him for life – and as he was living in a children's home at the time, he probably wasn't in an especially good place to begin with. We were just two people who collided with each other's lives for a split second. I still feel a bit bad about it, and wish I could go back in a time machine and at least push a note under his door saying sorry.

I force myself to stop procrastinating and open the door. Amazingly, nothing happens. No ghostly boys, no hanging corpses, no demons. Not even a whiff of the scary choir music from *The Omen*. It's just a room – dark, musty, and sad.

The desk I remember, covered in what I now think was probably dismantled computer parts or reverse-engineered toasters, has gone. The swivel-chair the boy spun around in has gone. There's nothing left here to tell me anything about the living, breathing children who once called this small place home.

I can feel the melancholy creeping back over me again, and shake it off. Nostalgia's not what it used to be, and I'm probably not well-equipped to deal with thinking too closely about the past. I struggle enough to cope with the present.

I wander over to the window, preparing to open it like I did all the others, and stop dead. Hazily outlined through the grime, I see a person standing outside. He's very still, looking up, probably thinking exactly the same thing as me: am I imagining this, or is there another human being out here in the land that time forgot?

I freeze for a moment, suddenly scared, and then use one of my cloths to wipe a circle of dirt from the window pane.

No, I'm not imagining it – it's a man. A tall man with dark hair, and a bloody big dog. I wave at him, and he hesitantly waves back. He can probably only see one bit of my face, which must look weird.

The dog lets out a vast booming woof, and I hear Bella's claws clattering on the floorboards in the hallway as she mobilises.

I follow her, fingering my mobile in my apron pocket for reassurance as I go. I generally don't go through life assuming new people I meet are serial killers – but Briarwood has cast its unnerving spell, and it's good to know I can communicate with the outside world if he suddenly wants to show me his stylish coat made of human skin.

I trot down the stairs, bundling up my bin bag as I go. Bella is ahead of me, her tail twitching in excitement. I am totally rocking the Cinderella look – face smeared with dirt, hair in a big mad pony, wearing a pinny that has a picture of King Kong on the front, odd socks popping out of the top of my Docs. Because life's too short for worrying about your socks.

I emerge into the sunshine, and have to blink away the sudden blast of light that attacks my indoor eyeballs.

It's been a surreal day. No sleep, domestic chaos, cleaning a haunted house, and now I'm standing out here, smiling at a man who definitely isn't Edward Cullen.

Chapter 3

Obviously, I knew that. Edward Cullen is a fictional character. This man, I assume, is not.

He's tall – a head higher than me, and I'm five-foot-ten – and he's wearing faded Levis and a T-shirt with Godzilla on it. The old black-and-white Godzilla, not the less-scary CGI Godzillas of the current era. His feet are bare – life is obviously too short for worrying about socks for him as well – and shoved into a pair of well-worn Converse with trailing, untied laces.

His hair is shorn close to his head, like he's either just left a super-secret post in the military or he knows from bitter experience that he'll end up with a huge 'fro if he lets it grow out. It looks soft and dark, like moleskin, and I know that I might need to fight the urge to stroke it. Because that would be weird for us both.

He's slender, but with broad shoulders and muscled arms that I'm guessing were created in a gym – he's too pale to be an outdoorsman. Dark brown eyes, strong cheek-bones and jaw, a nose that veers on the right side of Roman, a wide mouth. Beautiful, actually, in a you-could-use-him-as-a-sculpture-model kind of way. I see that the siren call of Budbury has resulted in yet another weird-but-well-built male responding to its pagan appeal.

'Hi!' I say, as I approach. For all I know he's worried that I'm a serial killer too. My appearance can be a little alarming to people I catch unawares. 'I'm Willow.'

He's not really focused on me, I realise as I get closer – he's staring at Bella, who has taken a few steps towards his dog, sniffed the air, and circled back to me. He has hold of his own pet's collar, and is looking anxious about the whole situation.

'Okay . . .' he replies, nervously. 'Any chance you could ask the dog to go back inside? Rick Grimes isn't too keen on company.'

Rick Grimes looks like a cross between a Rottweiler and a German Shepherd, with a face like a teddy bear, a hugely muscled body and a weird black-and-tan ruffle of fur around his neck, like a lion's mane. He's tugging slightly at his owner's hold, but not growling or snarling. Yet.

'You named your dog after a character in a TV show about zombies?' I ask, stepping in front of Bella protectively. I'm not overly worried – something about Bella gives off super-sexy vibes that generally ensure all male dogs adore her, the little tramp – but am ready to scoot her inside if I need to.

He looks up at me, and grins. It changes his whole face,

and something inside me melts a little. Danger, danger – hot geek alert.

'I did,' he says, stroking Rick's ears to soothe him as he talks. 'Why? What's your dog called?'

Hmmm. Fair question.

'Erm . . . Bella Swan,' I reply, feeling myself wilt a little. Not everybody gets the reference – but I am a hundred percent sure this guy will.

'Ah,' he says, his face creasing in amusement. 'Yes. That's a much more sensible name for a dog. If she had a puppy, would you call it Renesmee?'

'Don't be daft,' I answer. 'That's a stupid name for a dog.'

'Or a baby.'

'Yes, or a baby. I don't know what they were thinking . . . Rick Grimes looks like he's calmed down a bit now. Do you want to risk an introduction? Honestly, Bella's a bit of a femme fatale in the canine world. I've seen her tame the world's snarliest beasts with just one look. And she can run really fast when she wants to.'

I see him go through the possible outcomes in his mind: Rick falls in love with Bella and they live happily ever after creating puppies that have better names than Renesmee; Rick sniffs Bella's bum and they become BFFs 4 Eva; Rick tears Bella limb from fluffy limb and much carnage ensues.

In the end, Bella makes up his mind for him. Obviously sick of the stupid humans and their nonsense, she gets up and walks confidently towards Rick. She gives him a perfunctory sniff, and Rick quivers a little but endures it. Satisfied she now knows everything there is to know about him, Bella lies down, and curls up into a bored ball, one grey eyebrow raised at him in a provocatively nonchalant fashion.

This, I reckon, is where she always wins them over – with her sheer indifference. My friend Laura, from the café, has had two black Labs since I've known her. One, Jimbo, was a wonderful old gent who died not long after she moved here. Now, she has Midgebo, who is almost two but acts like a humungous puppy. Both dogs idolised Bella, while she simply pretends they don't exist in her universe.

The man crouches down beside Rick, and tentatively lets his grip on his collar loosen just enough for him to reach Bella, but still keeping enough of a hold to drag him back if he goes all hell hound on her.

Predictably enough, Bella works her magic – and within seconds, this giant of a dog is her slave, licking her all over like he's grooming her, before settling down next to her resting his enormous chin on her back. He closes his teddy bear eyes, and basically blisses out in the sunshine with his new crush.

'Wow,' Rick's owner says. 'I've never seen that before. If we're out anywhere in public I usually have to muzzle him. He loves people, especially kids – he licks their heads like lollipops – but goes psycho on other dogs. This is a definite first. Thank you.'

He sounds extremely grateful, and I congratulate myself

on having raised the dog version of Greta Garbo. I've learned to take small victories where I find them, in a life that sometimes feels full of whopping great defeats.

'You're welcome. Now that's sorted – what's your name?'

He stands up straight, and looks momentarily flustered, as he appears to really see me for the first time. The fluster turns into a frown as he takes in my appearance, and tries to figure it out.

'Oh! Sorry. Got so caught up in dog world I forgot my human life skill lessons . . . I'm Tom. Tom Mulligan. I'm the proud new owner of this place . . .'

He gestures towards Briarwood, and it crosses my mind that he's not much older than me – maybe thirty or so, if I had to guess. Even in its current state, this is a big house, sitting in a lot of land, and must have cost a decent whack. Maybe he's a millionaire philanthropist playboy, or an internet mogul, or a Lottery winner.

'Okay. Cool,' I say, not inquiring further. I'm feeling nosy on the inside though – my brain is constantly jam-packed full of questions, but my own life is complicated enough that I've learned not to always ask them.

Everyone has their story – especially people who seem to wash up here on our little corner of the coast – but not everyone immediately wants to share them. Anyway, give him five minutes alone with Cherie and Laura, and they'll have the lot out of him, pried from the depths of his soul by hook, crook and sticky buns. They're like the Spanish Inquisition, with cans of squirty cream.

He's staring at me quite intensely now, and clearly doesn't have quite enough social grace to hide his curiosity. More and more I am starting to sense that he's a man unused to much company, beyond himself and Rick Grimes.

'Are you . . . working here?' he asks, eventually, frowning.

'I am. Giving the place a clean to make it spic and span before the new owner gets here. Or at least that was the plan.'

'Right. Well, I hear the new owner's a bit of a dick, and does things like turn up a week before he should, and camps out in the woods in a motorhome just so he can get used to the place . . .'

A motorhome. Well, that at least clears up some of the mystery of how and why he was skinny-dipping in the pond this morning. Not that he needs to know about that.

'Your hair is a very, very bright shade of pink,' he says, after a moment's silence.

'I know,' I reply, fluffing up my pony tail with one hand. 'Flamingo chic – it's all the rage round here. Everyone in Budbury has bright pink hair.'

'That's not true, is it?'

'Not even a tiny bit. Anyway . . . it's been lovely to meet you, but I should probably get on. Those windows won't clean themselves.'

He nods, and casts his gaze back up to the third floor of the building. To the room where he'd first spotted me, staring out at him from my grimy perch.

I turn to go, wondering if Bella will follow or if she'll

stay and hang out with Rick Grimes a bit more. She pretends to be aloof, but I think she secretly loves all the attention.

'That used to be my room,' says Tom as I wave and walk away. He says it quietly, almost so quietly that I miss it.

I freeze, and blink my eyes a few times before I turn back to him. His room? *The* room? If he's about thirty, that'd make the age range right . . . wow. Could it actually be him? And if it is, how weird is all of this? I was literally only thinking about him minutes ago . . . again, I wonder if I've magicked him up. One minute he's Edward Cullen, the next minute he's the haunted room ghost boy from my childhood. I'd better be careful, or he might turn into the giant dough man from *Ghostbusters*.

He's still looking up at the window, and looks lost in time, as though he's being wrapped up in a blanket of memories. Much like I was not so very long ago. Something in his expression – wistful, melancholy, serious – tells me that a journey into the past is as unsettling for him as it was for me.

'Really?' I say, cautiously. I mean, I don't want to come across as any madder than I need to when I say this. 'When would that have been, about?'

'I starting living here after my parents died in a car crash. Late 1999. I left in 2003, when I was sixteen. It was . . . well, odd as it might sound, that was the most stable part of my life for a long time. Looks like Dracula's bachelor pad, I know, but it was a good place to live. The people who ran it were kind. They tried to give us what we needed. It wasn't their fault that they didn't have what I needed . . . Anyway. That's a million years ago, and not at all interesting to anyone but me. Sorry.'

He physically shakes his head, as though he's trying to dislodge the thoughts, and I massively sympathise with that. And I'm now also massively sure that this man – with his Godzilla T-shirt to complement my King Kong apron, and his crazy zombie-fighting dog, and his secret motor-home in the woods – is actually him. The Boy from the Room. Fate has brought us back together, and I'm glad that this time, at least, I didn't scream in his face and run away.

'This motorhome of yours,' I say, eventually. 'Does it come with a kettle?'

Chapter 4

From the outside, it looks like something the Famous Five would drive round in if they'd teamed up with the Scooby Doo gang. It's a vintage-looking VW camper van, with the distinctive spare wheel on the front and a raised roof space popped upright. One half is painted bright, shiny red, and the rest is a rich, gleaming shade of cream. And while it might look vintage, I can tell it's actually brand new from all the glistening chrome and this year's licence plate.

It's parked up in a clearing in the woodlands on the far side of the pond, a thick canopy of richly leaved trees hanging over and around it, sunlight streaming through the shade and reflecting off its glossy paint in strange, darting patterns.

It's a beautiful spot – I remember my mum telling me about the ancient hazel trees here, and how they've been added to with oak and ash, creating this idyllic corner of what is an already beautiful area. The floor is carpeted with bluebells and anemone, in swathes of lilac and white and yellow; butterflies with orange tips to their wings are fluttering around, and the air is drizzled with the sound of birdsong.

I pause, and breathe it in, letting the joy of it all filter through. It's all so green and perfect and warm.

'Isn't it exciting?' I say to Tom, turning to smile at him. 'How spring always comes around, every single year?'

He grins, and doesn't look alarmed, which is a good start. I can't help but feel happy, and the beauty of this luscious place is erasing the stresses and strains of the last couple of days. Many things might be wrong in the Willow-verse – but right here, right now, it all feels gorgeous.

'It is,' he answers. 'Even for an indoor boy like me. That's part of why I did this . . . bought this van, came here. I could stay in the posh hotel on the coast, but I wanted to try and . . . I don't know. Loosen up, I suppose.'

At first, I'm a little confused by that statement. I mean, he's wearing a Godzilla T-shirt and hasn't tied his shoelaces and has a dog called Rick Grimes. All the signs are pointing towards this guy being a mega-geek; one of those people who paints tiny figures of elves and goes to comic conventions.

Admittedly, he'd easily be the best-looking bloke at a comic convention – he could actually be an actor in one of those shows, like *Supernatural* or *The Vampire Diaries*, full of chiselled dudes with brilliant one-liners and tortured pasts. But still – he has that geeky vibe. Which is tradi-tionally not one that needs any loosening up.

But as soon as I follow him into the camper, leaving Bella and Rick outside to sniff interesting pieces of wood and chase caterpillars, I understand exactly what he means.

Outside, it looks hippy – expensive, but hippy. Pure retro. Inside, there's a completely different feeling. To say it's tidy would be an understatement. Everything is put away; the surfaces of the small table and cooking area are spotless; the pull-down bed is made with corners so sharp you could poke your eye out with them, and there's not a single sign of human habitation.

The front seats are covered in pristine cream leather, and the upholstery on the furniture looks brand new. Well, it is brand new – but if I'd been living here, it would all look a lot more messy by now.

There'd be a cereal box left out, or a book lying on the bed, or a pair of Doc Martens hanging from the ceiling, or some photos tacked up to the walls. I like my cleaning job – but in my own space, I like to be surrounded by a little bit of . . . well, me, I suppose.

After my mum's diagnosis, which was a long and torturous journey in itself, we were warned that she might lose some of her spatial awareness as the condition progressed, and find even familiar places difficult to navigate. We were told to expect bruised hips from hitting tables, or confusion about which way a door opened.

As it turns out, that hasn't happened – yet. She can still pull off advanced yoga poses, and is physically as fit as a fiddle. Not that I've ever figured out why a fiddle is especially fit, but there you go – one of life's many mysteries. But we did de-clutter the cottage a bit in anticipation – we did it together, on one of her very lucid days, so we wouldn't get rid of anything she'd later desperately want.

It didn't totally work. We had weeks of anguish where she was insisting someone had broken in and stolen her old knitting basket, even though I knew it had gone to the tip, but it does mean that the cottage is a lot less crowded than it used to be. Maybe that's why I still cling on to the random-ness of my own room.

Tom, I can see, is of the opposite persuasion. A man who looks like him, dresses like him, and uses the pop culture references he uses? I'd expect to see framed Han Solo quotes and possibly a display cabinet featuring original blaster guns from *Star Trek*. At the very least, a Spiderman tea-towel hanging from the cooker.

But no, it's all shipshape. A place for everything, everything in its place, almost untouched. It's such a contrast with the free-flowing wilderness outside – sterile and clean and man-made. If I'd only seen this and not the man himself, I'd say he definitely was in need of a little loosening up.

Maybe the skinny-dipping was part of that process – trying to recreate himself. If so, he'd come to the right place. Budbury, and especially the café where I work, specialises in second chances and fresh starts. A few of the people in our community are locals, but a lot of them are refugees from other places, and other times in their lives, looking for something different. Like Zoe, who runs the bookshop we've just opened – she moved here permanently in the new year with her goddaughter Martha, and Martha's dad Cal.

It's a long story, involving tragically early deaths, Australian cowboys and dysfunctional teenagers on the verge of rebelling themselves into oblivion – but now, it seems, they're all settled. Happy. Moving on with life. It's the Budbury Effect. Seriously, someone should do a scientific study on it. Maybe I will. I have a GCSE in Biology.

Tom, perhaps, will become the latest addition to the gang – or maybe he'll just stay long enough to do up Briarwood, sell it on at a vast profit, and bugger off again.

For the time being, he seems challenged enough by making a cup of tea. I can tell from his awkward, jerky movements that he's used to living alone, and not having to work around another human body. Each time we accidentally touch, he apologises, as though he's just invaded my personal space so much I might feel traumatised.

It doesn't bother me, but I can see that he's getting stressed. We're both stupidly tall, and the van isn't actually that big, even without any clutter – plus it's a glorious day out there.

'Why don't I go outside and leave you to it?' I say, taking pity on him. 'It's too nice a day to be cooped up inside anyway. It might be snowing tomorrow.'

He looks at me, and I see the relief he tries to hide.

'Good idea. There are some camping chairs out there. I

only use one, but they came as a set . . . I'll bring the tea out in a minute.'

I give him an enthusiastic thumbs up sign, and jump down onto the soft carpet of green at my feet. There's a bowl round the side, which Bella is drinking from while Rick – now reduced to a bit part in his own life – waits his turn, tongue lolling out and panting.

I take the opportunity to squat down and give his enormous head a stroke. His fur is so soft and dark, it feels like velvet beneath my fingers. I wonder where he sleeps, as I didn't see a dog bed in there. I have the sneaky suspicion that when it comes to his dog, Tom is maybe a bit less disciplined – I bet he sleeps curled up on the bed with him.

Rick gives my face a quick lick, and I set up the chairs. This takes a few attempts as the ground is uneven. I am unstable enough as it is, without deliberately setting myself off balance. Once I'm done, I sit quietly, legs stretched out in front of me, simply enjoying the warmth and the birdsong and the peace.

Moments like this are precious – knowing my mum is safely being looked after by the magical elfs at the café; knowing I'm exactly where I need to be, at the time I need to be there. One of the best coping mechanisms I've developed over the last couple of years has been this: just pausing and taking time to appreciate the way the world is at that exact moment, rather than fretting about a future I can't control or predict. I mean, by teatime it could all be different. I could be getting whacked round the head with a frying pan.

Tom emerges from the camper, ducking his head, and carrying two teas of steaming deliciousness. I always have a flask with me when I'm working, but it tastes even better when someone else has made it for you.

He sits next to me, settling himself carefully into the chair as though he expects it to collapse beneath his weight, and hands me the tea.

'It's beautiful here,' I say, stating the obvious.

'I know. It is. Taking a bit of getting used to, though – home is usually a flat on the top storey of a block in London. All mod cons. Night-time lullabies of sirens and car alarms. Rick prefers it here, but I've actually struggled a bit with the quiet since I arrived a couple of days ago.'

'Would you like me to arrange for some of the locals to come by and have a drunken argument outside at three a.m.?'

'Yes please,' he replies, smiling. 'And if you could persuade them to leave a half-eaten kebab on the doorstep and possibly smash a couple of bottles while they're at it, I'd feel even more at home.'

I nod sagely, and wonder who'd be up for it . . . any of them, I reckon. Maybe Becca and Sam. They've got a six-month old baby, Little Edie – little to differentiate her from her ninety-one-year-old namesake, Big Edie – so they're rarely asleep anyway. Plus Becca lived in her own flat in Manchester for years, so she'd probably have the urban nightscape routine down perfectly.

We look on as Bella decides to head into the camper van to investigate, followed quickly by her love toy. I raise my eyebrows to ask Tom if that's okay – some people are funny about that kind of thing – but he waves his hands in a 'no worries' gesture.

'When you go back in,' I say, sipping my tea, 'she'll be curled up asleep on your bed, and Rick will be on the floor, gazing up at her. She is now his Queen, and he is her subject. His life will never be the same again.'

'Well, he doesn't seem to mind. The fact that he's not gone for her throat or snarled at her shows that. It's a revelation – so long live the Queen. Anyway . . . how's it going, in the house? Making progress? I didn't really expect anyone to be cleaning it – I asked the estate agent to get someone to just make sure there weren't any dead bodies in cupboards, killer tarantulas in the cellar, that sort of thing.'

I involuntarily shudder a bit – it's the thought of the cellar – before I reply: 'Well, I get a lot of work like this, cleaning up places that have been empty a while. But this one . . . well, I'm sorting the windows so it's nice and bright, and I'll concentrate on the things you might keep, like the sinks and the lovely woodwork, but I'm guessing you might be planning on a refit anyway?'

I've phrased it like a question, and I hope I'm not being too nosy. Instead, he seems quite keen to talk about it.

'Where it's needed, yeah,' he says, gazing off into the distance while he thinks about it all. 'It's structurally sound

– I had all the surveys done – but I'd say there's probably a bit of a damp problem, and it all needs re-wiring, so the lights stop flickering on and off like something from a horror film. Did you notice that?'

'Only all the time,' I say, nodding. 'That would definitely be an improvement.'

'Plus I'd like to do some restoration work – the cornices and ceiling roses, some of the panelling; it all needs a bit of TLC. I'll redecorate, obviously, and sort out the gardens and the fountain. I used to love that fountain – I could see it from my window, and I'd watch the other kids playing out there all the time, jumping in and out of it in the summer, splashing each other. I could hear it at night as well, and it was . . . well, reassuring, I suppose. I need to find some local trades people to help with some of it, but I'm planning on doing at least part myself.'

'Right. Are you good at that kind of thing then?' I ask, knowing I'm frowning but not quite able to stop myself. 'DIY, I mean?'

'I can be, yes – why, don't I look like I am? Don't I look like a guy who could knock down a wall, or build an extension?'

He is pretending to be offended at this, as though I have somehow questioned his masculinity, but I can tell from the smile he's trying to hold down that he doesn't mean it.

'To be entirely honest . . .' I answer, smiling back. '. . . you look like the type of guy who can speak Klingon.'

'Maybe I can speak Klingon,' he responds. 'At least a few words. But I'm a Renaissance man – I also know my way around an angle grinder.'

'Well that's good – not to be obtuse, but I don't even know what an angle grinder is. I apologise profusely for implying that you were anything less than a rugged frontier man.'

He pauses before he replies, drinking his tea and kicking off his Converse, toes wriggling in freedom.

'Obtuse. Good gag. And truthfully? I'm not that rugged. I do understand the mechanics of houses, and the ways they work, and how to build them, but I've never actually done it. I started my career as a design engineer, and most of that involved being cooped up in a cubicle in a warehouse full of brainy nerds. Seriously, it was like that place where they hide the Ark of the Lost Covenant . . . loads of us, all really young and keen, beavering away, perfecting the essential next generation pencil sharpener or cat-flap or whatever.'

'Like *High School Musical* for Inventors?'

'A bit like that, yeah – but without the jocks or cheerleaders or cool kids. Just the nerdy ones. Eventually, after that and a few other jobs, I successfully invented something. I won't bore you with the details, but it was a part that's used in the manufacture of small spherical objects. Like ball bearings, or beads, or a few of the items used in plumbing . . .'

I pretend to snore, and let my head loll to one side as

though I'm asleep. After a second or two, I jolt back 'awake', careful not to spill my tea during the whole charade.

'Sorry!' I say, brightly. 'You lost me at ball bearings . . .'

'Ha ha,' he snarks back, kicking my ankle in retaliation. 'You are so hilarious.'

'I know, right? I should do stand-up. Anyway . . . so why the move here? Why leave your city idyll and escape to the country?'

'I don't know. Ask me that in a few months' time. I was site-surfing one day, and came across this place and recognised it. "Small Victorian manor house," it said, "in need of some renovation." I did a bit of digging – not actual digging, you understand, my milky-white skin is far too delicate for that – and found out it'd been sitting empty for all these years. It made me . . . well, it made me sad. Like I said, I was actually happy here – as happy as I could've been, under the circumstances – and I hated the thought of it being neglected. Stupid, I know – sentimental and stupid. It's a house, not a person. Now you probably think I'm nuts, as well as a pathetic city slicker nerd.'

Wow. That's quite a speech. I suddenly get the impression that this is the first time he's tried to put all of this into words – or at least spoken those words to anyone other than Rick Grimes, who probably isn't that chatty.

I put my mug down on the grassy floor, and it immediately falls over. Huh. At least it was empty.

'I have to be honest,' I say, eventually, glancing over and noticing that he isn't meeting my gaze. Maybe a bit embarrassed. 'That doesn't even come close to being nuts in this village. You're going to have to try an awful lot harder if you want to fit into that category. You'll understand what I mean when you meet everyone . . . which you will, I guarantee. If you don't come to the village, the village will come to you.'

'Will they bring flaming torches and buckets of pitch?'

'No, they'll bring carrot cake and caramel macchiatos and possibly a whole spit roast suckling pig. And then they'll show you what nuts really is, in the nicest way you can imagine. And . . . no, it really doesn't sound nuts. I know exactly what you mean. This place is special to you, and you care about what happens to it. That's lovely, not nuts.'

He nods, but doesn't look entirely convinced. By my response, or the thought of the proposed invasion of the village people.

'I'm not that good,' he says, slowly. 'With big groups. With people I don't know. Or people I do know . . . just people, really. I'm okay with dogs, and with machines, and technology. People? Not my strong suit. Not to sound too macho, but they scare the shit out of me. I just don't understand normal people.'

'Ah, well that's where you're in luck – none of these people are normal. You'll be fine, I promise. And you seem okay with meeting me.'

He looks at me, and grins. He looks stupidly handsome, and it's hard to reconcile the way he looks with what he is – a socially awkward nerd-man. In another life, he could have been something entirely different. Like an actor or a politician or one of those people who model for romance book covers.

'I do seem okay with you, don't I?' he says, laughing. 'Weird. I think it's because you own a magical dog named after something even lamer than mine. And you have pink hair, and dress a bit like Doctor Who's assistant.'

I glance down at my Docs – silver spray-painted – and my odd socks and the tattered fishnet tights I have on beneath the socks, popping out beneath my Minions leggings. Right. He has a point there.

'Plus, you seem so relaxed,' he adds. 'Like you could sit in these woods all day drinking tea and chatting to a stranger. Like you don't have a care in the world.'

'Yep,' I reply, shrugging. It would be cruel to spoil his illusion with the nitty-gritty of my life. 'That's me. Little Miss Sunshine. Anyway . . . I can't sit here all day, and I have a confession to make. I don't think we're strangers. I think we've actually met before.'

'No way,' he says quickly, looking confused. 'I'd definitely have remembered you.'

'I didn't have pink hair back then,' I answer, easing myself into the subject. 'In fact, I was only eight, and you were a few years older. It was summer – maybe the first one you'd been at Briarwood – and . . . well, maybe you don't remember. But one day, my brothers and sister convinced me the room you lived in was haunted, and they dared me to come in and find out for myself. So I opened the door, and you – I think it was you – were sitting there, at your desk, making something, which does add up now. And then . . .'

'And then you screamed your head off, and ran away! That was you? Really?'

'Yes. That was me. So you remember that, do you?'

'Remember? I was scarred for life. I should probably have had counselling. In a bad year, it was one of the absolute highlights. My parents were dead, the rest of my family was . . . well, unavailable. I was living here, surrounded by other kids I had nothing in common with and couldn't talk to, and then *you* happened. A screaming little whirling dervish. I'm lucky I didn't drop dead that second. I saw you later . . . you were with those other kids, weren't you? Your mum worked at Briarwood?'

By this stage, I'm holding my face in my hands, partly in shame and partly in amusement. I'd always suspected that incident all those years ago was a bit like the thing grown-ups says when you see a spider – it's more scared of you than you are of it.

'I'm so sorry,' I wheeze out between laughs. 'Honestly, I am. I was thinking about it today – I was actually a bit scared to go into that room, and I was feeling guilty, about freaking you out like that. What can I say? I'm the youngest of four. They were evil, and they made me do it. And yes . . . my mum worked there. You may have enjoyed one of her chakra-cleansing workshops at one stage or another.'

'Definitely not,' he replies firmly, grinning at the memory. 'That would have involved leaving my room. Although she did visit me up there sometimes, tried to get to know me. She was pretty intuitive actually – brought me technical drawing pads instead of sketch pads, and gave me books with weird inventing stuff in them. She tried with *Frankenstein*, but when that didn't catch she brought me biographies – George Stephenson, Isambard Kingdom Brunel. You know, your average cool kid stuff . . . but she was nice. I was just too wrapped up in myself back then to respond properly. Is she . . . you know, still around?'

He says this tentatively, knowing that we have reached the age where it's not always a given.

I nod enthusiastically. 'Oh yes! Very much so. And I'm glad she helped . . . maybe it'll offset some of the bad family karma I earned by making you poo your pants.'

I stand up, planning to get back to work – plus avoid any more questions about my mother, as that's too big and too private a subject for now – and he stands next to me. He's so tall I have to look up at him, which is an unusual feeling for me. I don't entirely hate it.

'I didn't poo my pants,' he replies, as we walk back to the camper van. 'I'd just like to state that for the record.'

'Noted and recorded. I'll add it to the typed transcript of this conversation when I next see my secretary.'

We climb up into the van with empty mugs in hand, and sure enough, Bella is flat out on the bed. She's fast asleep, all four paws sticking out, jerking slightly as she dreams. Rick is squashed into the remaining floor space, his gaze turned towards Bella and only Bella.

'Shit,' says Tom, taking in the scene. 'He was my one friend in the world – and he's abandoned me for a vampire Border Terrier.'

Chapter 5

I picked my mum up from the café, where she was reading poetry out loud to Edie May, staying only long enough to give everyone a quick update on the House on the Hill, and eat some cake. I'm busy, but there's always time for cake. I was peppered with so many questions I could barely spoon my Black Forest Gateau in. I kept it mysterious, just for fun – I rarely know more than the ladies at the café do, so I enjoy my brief moment of power.

After that brief and calorific restorative, we came home for our tea. My mum, Lynnie, is lying on the sofa, with her latest notepad creation spread in front of her. She goes to a day centre twice a week, and they helped her make her new cover.

Not everyone takes to this kind of thing but it was practically invented for her. She was always one of those women who could whip up a fancy dress outfit for school from an old curtain, a roll of tin foil and some paperclips.

The first page is, as always, taken up with the practical information that helps her get through the challenges of her day. The rest will, bit by bit, become filled with memories, thoughts, and notes. I try to respect her privacy, but I do occasionally crack and sneak a peek – usually if she's been particularly agitated or too quiet, both of which are signs that something is wrong and she either doesn't feel comfortable talking to me about the problem, or simply can't quite find the words to explain herself.

The cover of this one is decorated with the glued-on petals of pressed flowers she's been squashing between the pages of her weird hardback books about stone circles for days now. It's a bright collage of cow parsley, bluebell, foxglove, wood sorrel and the beautiful pale yellow trumpets of wild daffodil. It's like spring time has come alive on the page, and I almost expect butterflies to fly out from the folds.

She's shielding the pages as she writes, and glancing up at me every now and then, looking slightly suspicious. One of the many joys of Alzheimer's is that it can be so unpredictable. Some days, she's pretty much like her old self – bouncing around with loads of energy, burning incense in the garden, telling me off for using toxic chemicals on my hair. She doesn't mind the nose ring I sometimes wear, or the Celtic tattoos I have on my arms, but the thought of the hair dye really bugs her.

I relish those days. I love getting told off by my mum, which are words I never thought I'd hear myself say when I was a teenager. But getting told off by her means she knows exactly who I am, and who she is, and what our roles are.

Other times, it's not so simple. It's not always like in the movies, where she has no clue who I am – well, it is sometimes. Like when she hits me with a frying pan and tells the police I'm a burglar. But that's relatively rare, and I can usually spot the build-up in the days before one of those episodes. A lot of the time, it's somewhere in between – she knows she feels safe with me, and that I'm important, but isn't 100 percent sure why.

Those days are hard on her – and on me. I can almost see her poor brain struggling to make the connection, fighting against its degeneration to put all the clues together. She seems embarrassed by it – as though she knows she's missing something big, and it makes her feel helpless and useless and . . . well, just 'less' in general.

That's one of the reasons the notebooks are useful. When I see her doubts, see the way she's trying to hide her uncertainty, I can open that front page, and point to it, and watch as she reads it through. There's always a moment when it clicks into place, when her face breaks out into a joyful smile that makes me want to weep – the moment she remembers. When she knows she is here with me, her daughter, who loves her, and who she loves in return.

Tonight, I can tell she's not completely sure of herself. I still have an egg-shaped reminder of the frying pan incident, and am not keen to repeat it, so I quietly sit down on the chair opposite her, and casually say: 'That's a really beautiful notebook. Did you make that at the day centre?'

'I did – with my friend Carole,' she replies politely, moving fluidly into an upright position on the couch, holding the book on her knees. She's very slim, my mum, with long, lean limbs that are still sinewy from years of yoga and exercise. Even though her hair is striped different shades of grey, it's still thick and curly, and frames what is even now a very pretty face. She's sixty-five, but has the kind of looks it's hard to date – she could be anywhere between forty-five and seventy-five, depending on the light and her mood.

'Carole's really nice,' I say in return. It helps if we build up gradually as we talk. 'When I dropped you off at the centre yesterday, she was waiting outside for you, wasn't she? I think maybe she's had her hair done.'

'She has! You're right. She's gone blonder. Do you know Carole too?'

'I do, yes. We're all friends. I'm glad she helped you do that new book. Did she help you fill in the first page as well? Why don't you have a look at it?'

I can tell she's thinking I'm a bit doo-lally – this is a common and ironic occurrence – but she indulges me, and reads over the front page.

I see her take in the words, and look at the pictures, and cast surreptitious glances across at me. I see the moment she joins the dots, and the moment when she hides the fact that she was ever confused in the first place.

Like I say, she gets embarrassed, as though her problems are a sign of weakness rather than because the nerve cells in her brain are refusing to cooperate any more.

I let her believe she's fooled me, that everything is fine – because why wouldn't I? She doesn't have many places to seek refuge any more. This illness is laying her bare, bit by bit, and if she finds it consoling to sometimes pretend it's not happening, then I'm not going to be the voice of doom.

Sometimes I have to be firm – like when she decides she's going to book a place on a yoga retreat in Nepal, or take a road trip to visit the parents she sometimes forgets are dead – but not tonight. Not right now.

'Guess what I did today, while you were at the café?' I say brightly, hoping to distract her from her burgeoning self-loathing.

'I have no idea,' she replies, crossing her legs easily into lotus, and giving me one of her glorious smiles. 'What did you do today?'

'I went to the House on the Hill to do some work. Do you remember it – Briarwood? Mr and Mrs Featherbottom? All the children who used to live there?'

'Of course I remember it!' she replies, sounding astounded that I would even question such a thing. 'I was there over the summer last year, wasn't I? Holding those workshops? So many precious young people, all needing so much love . . .'

In fact, it's been well over a decade since she worked

57

Debbie Johnson

there – but it's not uncommon for her timeline to get a bit mixed up. It's like she's living in an especially complicated episode of *Quantum Leap*. I know she remembers Briarwood, and remembers it fondly, because it's one of the places on her Wanderlust List. Every now and then, she goes walkabout, often after being agitated in the late afternoon. Usually she'll take an unplanned and unaccompanied trip back in time.

She'll walk to the café on the clifftops, or to the Community Centre in the village, and sometimes even persuade people that they need to take part in a yoga class. I once found her in the café, putting Laura in a downward dog over breakfast. She's tried to make it to Briarwood a few times, but as it's quite a way off and up that big hill, she usually either gets spotted and someone calls me, or gives up and comes home, covered in mud or scratches from hedgerows. So far, no harm has come from any of this – but it is always terrifying, the realisation that she's gone.

It leaves me wracked with guilt as well, even though logically I know that I can't watch her twenty-four hours a day – I need sleep, and rest, or I won't be able to function at all.

'I think,' I reply, gently, 'that it might have been a bit longer ago than that, Mum. But it doesn't matter – anyway, someone has bought the house. One of the boys who used to live there.'

'Really?' she asks, frowning in confusion. 'Have Mr and

58

Mrs Featherbottom left, then? They worked so hard, those two . . . but it's a lot to ask isn't it, looking after so many damaged children? I do what I can to help them, but there are some you can never quite reach.'

'I'm sure you helped a lot of them, Mum. This one certainly remembers you as being really nice to him. He's called Tom, and he's an inventor.'

'Oooh! How exciting! What did he invent?'

She claps her hands together as she says this, delighted at the very thought.

'Umm . . . I'm not quite sure what it's called,' I reply, honestly. 'Something to do with industry, and making things. Ball bearings, I think.'

'Shall we call it a flange bracket?' she says, her eyes twinkling mischievously. For a moment, she's back to being my brilliant, whacky, never-at-all-boring mother – the mother who made up stories for us at bedtime instead of reading them, and who always had an alternative word to hand. Cornflakes were crack-of-dawn-flakes; pyjamas were llamas; cuddles were muddles. There were so many of them – it was as though she had her own form of rhyming slang, or a type of Edward Lear-style nonsense language.

'Yes!' I say enthusiastically. 'I think that's the perfect word for whatever it is. He invented a flange bracket, and made a lot of money from it, and now he's bought Briarwood.'

She's silent for a moment, stroking the pressed flower petals on the front of her notebook. She looks up at me, and asks: 'Are you going there tomorrow? Or to the café?'

'Possibly both. You can go and see Carole again, if you like.'

I never force her to go to the day centre – her life choices are narrowing rapidly now, so I try to give her as many as I can. There's funding for two days a week there, but she doesn't always use them. We work around it. There's a local agency that provides carers, and a lady called Katie who moved to the village a while ago sometimes comes and sits with her.

Katie used to be a nurse, and is now a single mum to her almost-three-year-old, Saul – she doesn't want to go back to work yet, but helping me and Mum out keeps her busy. The added bonus is that Mum adores Saul and he thinks she's some magical witch, so it works well. Other times, she comes with me, depending on what I'm up to.

She's turning it over in her mind, and I hope she chooses Carole. It's late to ask Katie for help, and having seen the state of Briarwood, I'm not sure it would do her any good at all. It was weird enough for me, even though I'm aware of the passage of time. If she arrives there thinking it's the summer of 2006 or something, she'll be completely freaked out by it its ruined condition.

'Yes,' she says finally. 'Carole. But maybe one day, you can take me to the House on the Hill again? I'd like to meet the famous inventor of the flange bracket.'

'You will, I promise,' I say, yawning halfway through the words. 'He's really nice.'

Mum stands up and stretches, long and tall. She yawns too, and I realise we are both exhausted.

'Time to turn in?' I ask, raising my eyebrows. She nods, and comes over to give me a cuddle – or a muddle, depending on your word choice. I sink into her arms, and let my head loll on her shoulder, and close my eyes.

Just for a minute, I let myself forget – forget the real world, and all its problems. Forget that I am the carer and she is the one in need of care. I forget everything, and just allow myself to feel like a little girl, safe and content in her mum's arms at the end of a busy day.

'Love you, Pillow,' she says, dropping a kiss on my head and leaving the room. Pillow. That wasn't one of her nick-names for me – it's just one of the words that seem to have got messed up on the way from her brain to her mouth. She's probably thinking about bed, so that makes sense.

'Love you, Mum,' I reply as she pads off to her room at the end of the corridor. 'Sleep well.'

I stay in the chair for a few minutes – it is super squishy and comfy – and let my mind wander. I make a little check-list of all the things I have yet to do, before forcing myself to my feet to actually do them. If I sit for even a minute longer, I'll actually fall asleep. I'll wake up at 4 a.m. with some bonkers infomercial for ab-crunching exercise machines on the TV, my hair glued to my cheeks and my eyes stuck together with gunk.

Sighing, I push myself upright, and start my usual

Bedtime Patrol. I switch off the TV, and have a very perfunctory tidy-up, mainly picking anything from the floor up and putting it away. Removing trip hazards has become a way of life, as much for me when I'm walking round half-asleep as anything.

I check the windows are locked with the little keys, which I keep in my room with me. Same with the front door, and the back door. It feels weird – as though I'm keeping my mum a prisoner – but I just can't rest if I think she's going to sneak out. I mean, she does anyway sometimes – she'll remember where I keep them and find a way to get them in the night. Mostly she doesn't, but I feel better if they're close to hand. I should probably invent a flange bracket that keeps them safer.

I go into the kitchen, my favourite place in the house, to get ready for the morning. It's a big room, with an old stone-flagged floor that's been worn shiny by generations' worth of feet traipsing across it. The ceiling is a bit on the low side, and beamed, but I know it's high enough to avoid me banging my head unless I'm on a pogo-stick or wearing stilettos – neither of which I am often doing.

The sink is a massive, ancient Belfast affair, and the surfaces are all made of thick old slabs of pine. It's a kitchen that's been well-used and well-loved, for a long time.

Outside, through the window with its blue gingham curtains, I can't see much now – it might have been a beautiful day, but it's still only spring, and it's already dark out there in the wilds.

In the daylight, though, it's a beautiful view. Our cottage is on the edge of Frank's farm, and all you can see beyond our garden is fields, stretching for miles in myriad shades of green. Our own garden used to be spectacular – Mum was a dab hand – but now we try and keep it simple.

She still has her vegetable patch, but is hit and miss with how much interest she has in it. Frank often comes round to tend to it himself, pretending he does it purely for the fresh fruit and veg we pay him with. I know that's not true – Frank has a whole farm to himself. I know it's just a kindness and I accept it, gratefully. I like to be as independent as I can, but weeding when you don't need to is taking independence too far.

There's a bench and a table and a couple of old chairs out there, positioned so you can watch the sunset over the hills, and even a scarecrow that has been there longer than we have. He's called Wurzel, and when we were kids we used to dress him up for the different seasons – a Santa hat at Christmas, monster mask at Halloween, that kind of thing. I remind myself to find something gorgeous and spring-like for him to wear very soon. Maybe a daffodil-shaped hat, or a jaunty Easter bonnet.

I get everything ready for the next day. I place two bowls, two spoons, and a big tub of Laura's home-made granola on the table, along with two mugs. Too many questions can confuse Mum first thing in the morning, not to mention myself, so I try to plan ahead and keep it simple for both of us.

I make sure the 'Monday' section of her pill box is empty, and check that everything is stocked and ready to go for Tuesday – she doesn't always like to take her medication, but as they've yet to find a way to alleviate Alzheimer's through a nice ginger tea and a nettle poultice (her traditional approach to healing), it's a small battle we have to face regularly. Some days she's absolutely fine about it – others, for some reason, she's not. She'll hide them, or even hold them in her mouth and pretend she's swallowed. Those are fun times.

I wipe down the counters, and change the sheet on the page-a-day calendar. It's huge, and plainly printed black-on-white, and the alleged idea is to provide a simple reminder of what date it is without having to try too hard. Of course, that depends on me remembering to tear the old pages off.

I check the dryer, and fold out a load of laundry into the basket. Mum will get up and usually comes through into the kitchen in her llamas, at which point I'll sneak into her room and lay out some clothes, in the order she needs to put them on – knick-knacks and bra, then socks, and whatever else she's wearing.

She doesn't always take notice, and emerges wearing something completely different instead – and who can blame her? It's every woman's right to choose a fuchsia feather boa and hounds-tooth tweed jacket combo if she wants to. As long as it's weather-appropriate and covers her modesty, I don't really care. Nobody would ever accuse me of making conservative choices on the wardrobe front, that's for sure.

Once I've sorted the clothes, I make sure Bella's water bowl is full, and tucked under the table where it's out of the way. She watches me from the corner of the room, tail twitching, knowing the bedtime ritual by now. I switch off most of the lights, leaving small plug-in night-lights on just in case Mum gets up while I'm asleep.

Bella follows me to the back door, where I stand and wait while she does her night-time business, before locking up again and going to attend to my own. By the time I've brushed my teeth and changed into a pair of mis-matched llamas, I'm ready to fall asleep standing up. I am pathetic-ally grateful for the fact that our cottage is all on one level, and I don't have to face stairs. I wouldn't make it without a Sherpa.

I fall onto the bed, pausing for a second to enjoy the silence, the peace, and the feel of all my things around me, before scuttling under the duvet. My pillowcase smells of lavender, which means Mum has been housekeeping – and sure enough, I find a dried sprig tucked inside it. I smile, and put it back. Every now and then she does that, or leaves fresh wildflowers in my room, or writes me a rude limerick and pins it to my headboard. She is still, even in this constantly changing version of herself, really rather brilliant.

I glance at the clock on the nightstand, and let out a self-mocking snort. Willow Longville. Party animal.

Completely exhausted and already tucked up in bed – at 8.38 p.m.

Bella waits until I'm settled, then leaps nimbly up onto the bed. She circles several times, then curls up in a ball right next to my head, as though she's a human claiming the other pillow.

I let my hand rest on the warm fur of her back, and feel the comforting rise and fall of her breath. I wonder if she'll dream about Rick Grimes. And I wonder if I'll dream about Tom Mulligan, the famous inventor of the even-more famous flange bracket.

I may fall asleep pathetically early, but I do at least fall asleep with a smile on my lips.

Chapter 6

I finish polishing the banister and stand back to admire it. I've used a beeswax mixture, and the wood feels soft and smooth and silky beneath my fingers. I lean forward and take a quick sniff – divine. It smells like honey, and would be Winnie the Pooh's most favourite banister in the whole world.

I walk up to the next floor, and stroke the big, oval wooden ball, which I note with satisfaction I can now see my face in. A weird, stretched bit of my face, but all the same it feels good to have helped Briarwood heal a little.

There's one of these oval wooden balls at the end of each curving level, and although they may well have a proper name, I always think of them as the Pineapple-Shaped Bottom-Stoppers.

With hindsight, sliding down these banisters was probably dangerous. But a big house full of kids is always going to present a health and safety challenge, and I know I spent many happy hours whizzing up and down them. As soon as I finished the full set of slides, I'd gallop back up all the stairs with that endless fizzing energy that very young people have.

By that stage, only Angel was still keeping me company on the slide-a-thon, and even then only when the older two weren't looking. Auburn was way too cool for such nonsense at fourteen, and Van had given up that particular vice after a close encounter with one of the Pineapple-Shaped Bottom-Stoppers left him near-crippled in the goolies department. I fear I may have screeched with laughter on that occasion, as he rolled around the floor cupping his precious man-parts.

It's odd, remembering all of this. Some of it – the practicalities of day-to-day life, school, bedtime, boring stuff – is hazy. But other scenes are crisp and clear, frozen in time like little tableaux, as though they've been captured for posterity in my brain: carved into it like those little frescos of Roman Gods you see in museums. Except we'd be Roman street urchins, with smudged faces and tattered togas.

I'm still stroking the wood when I hear the familiar 'woof' that announces the presence of Rick Grimes, and the sound of footsteps on the floorboards as Tom follows him into the building. He looks up, and I pop my head over the rail, waving.

'Hellooooo down there!' I shout, as Rick gallops up the stairs three at a time to be reunited with Bella. 'I'm just upstairs, fondling wood!'

He raises his eyebrows and smirks, and I realise a nanosecond too late how that one sounded. Ah well. C'est la vie.

Tom makes his way up towards me, and I note with satisfaction that he also can't help himself – his fingers are caressing the mahogany as he goes.

'Your fingers will smell of honey now,' I say, as he makes it to the top.

'Could be worse,' he says, shrugging, and looking on in amusement as Rick runs from room to room, sniffing the ground until he finds the one she's snoozing in. I don't know if dogs are capable of subterfuge, but if they are, she's definitely pretending to be asleep right now.

Tom looks down at the staircase, and sniffs the air appreciatively.

'Thanks for this, Willow,' he says, sincerely. 'It's already feeling much better in here. I know it'll probably all get covered in dust and sawdust during the work, but I'm glad to see at least a bit of it coming back to life. Does that make sense?'

'Well, it makes sense to me,' I reply, screwing the lid back on the beeswax as I talk. 'But I have famously low standards when it comes to making sense. I've finished all the windows, cleaned all the sinks in the boys' bedrooms, and given all the hallways a sweep. Before I waste my time buffing floorboards or anything, why don't you tell me a bit more about what you're planning to do? I'd be really interested in hearing it anyway.'

'Really? You would? Haven't you got anything better to be doing?'

'Well, I was supposed to be adjudicating a naked mud

bath wrestling contest between Ryan Reynolds and Ryan Gosling this lunch time . . .'

'Ah. To see which one wins the Ultimate Battle of the Ryans?'

'That's the one. But I can put them off until another time. Besides, they'll never beat the Ultimate Battle of the Bruces – Willis vs Lee. That was a real humdinger. Karate chops, sub-machine guns, vest tops, the lot.'

'Wow. Yippe-kay-ay, motherfucker,' he replies, doing a more-than-passable John McClane impression. He leans down, and helps me gather all the cloths and dusters together. I pack them back into the bag I wear tied stylishly around my waist, and pause to admire his Goonies T-shirt as I do so. He has his Converse tied today, and his dark hair looks damp. I wonder if he's been in the pond again, but don't ask.

'Well,' he says, walking along the corridor and gesturing for me to follow. 'I'm not entirely sure yet. I don't even really know what I'm going to do with the place. It's too big for me on my own, but I'm hardly in a position to fill it with friends and family, being a poor little orphan boy with a limited social circle. I suppose I'm still playing with ideas – mainly, using it as a retreat for young geniuses in need of free board and lodging, away from the temptations of the bright lights and wi-fi?'

'Okay. Like, some kind of charity for brainiacs?'

'Yeah, I suppose so . . . I mean. I have the money. It's not like I've blown it all on Aston Martins and private jets.

I have four patents that have paid off, and a couple more pending. I've already come up with a few more ideas since I've been here – basically because there's nothing much else to do. So if it's had that effect on me, it might work for others.'

I nod, and follow him along the hallway. He peeks into the rooms, smiling wryly as we look into the one that used to be his, and I practically see the cogs of his super-tuned brain turning. He's almost purring with intellect, which is strangely sexy.

'I think I'll have to get some of the floorboards replaced,' he says, as we make our way down the stairs again. 'Some will be okay if they're sanded down and polished. Once the damp-proofing's sorted, and I've had the roof looked at, I can start properly.'

'And this . . .' he says, as we reach the big main hallway and lobby area. 'This just needs a really good redesign. There's loads of space, but it still feels a bit dark and oppressive. I think I might knock through those little rooms there – the ones that used to be the cloakrooms – and open it all out a bit. Then there's the big hall, which we used as a dining room – it's huge, but gloomy. I need to fix that.'

He carries on talking me through his ideas, sometimes adjusting them as he goes, and I actually start to see it: a complete facelift that manages to keep the building's sense of history and character, but fills it with light and fresh purpose. He comes to life as he speaks, and so do his hands – he's waving them around, gesturing at the ceiling, pointing into rooms, opening doors and gesticulating. He's lost in his own imagination, and it seems to be a good place.

'What about the office and the living quarters?' I ask, as we approach the end of the hallway. I can still half imagine Mr and Mrs F in here, whiling away their nights singing Gilbert and Sullivan operettas to each other by the light of the silvery moon.

'Not sure . . .' he replies, frowning as he looks into the abandoned room. Its 'life, interrupted' vibe is still quite heavy, and I decide to tackle this part of the house next. 'I don't know if I'll be staying, or just setting it all up and heading back to London.'

'Ah. The irresistible allure of the kebab shops and tube stations?'

'More the irresistible allure of what I'm used to, I suppose. It's amazing how much solitude you can find in a place like London – literally millions of people, but not a single one interested in you at all. That's what I'm used to.'

'Well if you stay here for any length of time, you'll need to get used to the opposite – literally dozens of people, and every single one of them fascinated by you. Talking of which, you should come to the café. I'm thinking tomorrow, after the lunch rush – by which I mean eight people eating ham toasties. Come along and meet everyone. It'll happen sooner or later. Might as well get it over with.'

He shuffles from foot to foot, rifling through the old paperbacks, nodding vaguely but not actually answering. It doesn't take telepathic powers to realise he's about as keen on that idea as having all his teeth removed without anaesthetic.

'I'm not sure,' he says, when I prompt him by poking him on the back of the head with a feather duster. 'I mean . . . I couldn't leave Rick alone for long, could I?'

'Bring him with you,' I reply, and immediately hold my hand up to stop his flood of objections. 'And yes, I know what you said about him – and I believe you. I fully accept that his love for Bella might not translate to all his other doggy interactions. But it'll be quiet, and the only other dog who's likely to be there is Midgebo, Laura's black lab. If Rick shows signs of wanting to eat him, he can stay outside – there's a whole field for dogs, set up with water bowls and rest spots, like a canine crèche.'

Tom doesn't look convinced, and I don't know why I'm insisting – I hate it when people try and get me to do things I don't want to. I usually start speaking fake Japanese at them and pretending I don't understand. But there's just something about Tom that makes me think that if he broke through his own reluctance, and at least tried, then spending some time at the café with the Budbury massive would be good for him.

I realise even as I think this how annoying it is – everyone who tries to get you to do something 'for your own good' always thinks they're right, don't they? Including me, apparently.

'Look, you don't have to – I get it. You're happy out here in the woods, going all Grizzly Adams, enjoying your back to nature trip. But honestly? They're all lovely. I'm probably the most repulsive and disgusting of them all – everyone else is way nicer than me.'

He turns around to face me, and he's grinning. Maybe – just maybe – changing his mind might not be out of the question.

'I'll think about it,' he says. 'As long as they're not as repulsive and disgusting as you. I presume there will be cake?'

'The most majestic cake found in this galaxy or any other.'

'And there won't be too many people? If I try and over-load my geek brain with too many real people – as opposed to imaginary ones in fantasy novels – my head might explode. I'm too pretty for that to happen.'

He says that mockingly, but he is handsome – just not in a way I suspect he's ever really thought about. He's all about the mind, this guy – but the mind is housed in a not-too-shabby package.

'There won't be too many real people, no. But . . . hey, I have an idea! Would it help if I made you a fact file? If you can keep all the different houses in *Game of Thrones* straight, I'm sure you can manage this. I could do you a round-up in advance, and you could . . . I don't know, make yourself a spreadsheet or whatever it is people like you do to process information?'

'Usually I just insert the memory card directly into my biological data portal.'

'I'm not even going to ask where that is . . .'

He winks at me in an exaggerated 'Carry On' fashion, which makes me laugh out loud.

'But yes,' he continues, looking slightly more serious. 'Something like that probably would help me, a bit. I'd feel less like I was walking into a booby trap, and it might stop me doing this brilliantly cool thing I do where I stare at my own feet and walk into walls.'

'That's all right. We won't mind if you do . . . but if you think it'll help, I'll do it tonight. I'll just cancel that Ultimate Battle of the Hughs – Jackman vs Grant – and write an epic account of life in Budbury. Give me your email address before I leave.'

I glance at my watch and see that I should actually be leaving pretty soon. It's almost a thirty-mile round trip to get my mum from the day centre, and I have to help Laura cover the lunch shift at the café as well. The rock and roll never stops.

'I need to be going soon,' I say to Tom, who immediately nods and looks business-like again. 'But before I leave, promise me one thing . . .'

'Maybe. What is it?' he frowns, looking a tiny bit suspicious.

'You know you said one of the reasons you came here was to try and loosen up a bit?'

'Ye-es . . .'

'Well, I'm a bit of an expert in loosening up, and I have a task for you. Perhaps see me as your chilling-out doctor, and this as your first lesson in your free-spirit quest.'

He narrows his eyes, and waits for me to continue, obviously not willing to commit himself until he hears what my first prescription is.

'This afternoon, Mr Mulligan, I want you to go to the top floor of this house – and slide all the way down on the banisters.'

He puffs out a quick breath, and shakes his head.

'No way. I was never the kind of kid who did things like that.'

'Well maybe,' I say over my shoulder as I walk out of the room, 'it's about time you were!'

Chapter 7

My mum senses that a new project is afoot, and joins me at the kitchen table. I have my laptop open, and am working on the Budbury Bible for Tom. I'm also quite excited, now I've started – this will be a lovely keepsake for the future: a snapshot of life in the village as it is right now. A lot of our residents are elderly, and despite the fact that they all seem in exceptionally good health, they won't be around forever.

I'm also maybe more aware than others of the value of these records. Now, at this stage in my life, I have no problems with memory or mental confusion beyond my normal accepted levels – I've always been on the fuzzy side, and that's okay.

But one day, this might matter – I might be able to look back at it and remember all the brilliance that went on. We all take so much for granted, and if my mum's situation has taught me anything, it's not to make that mistake.

It also makes me realise what a weird and wonderful collection of people we have here. Everyone is different, and different is okay – some people throw themselves into a new social situation with ease and openness, like Laura did when she first moved here. Others, like Tom, are practically paralysed with fear at the prospect. We're all different, we're all flawed – and there's a place for everyone. Or at least there should be.

'What are we doing, Willow?' Mum asks, sliding her chair in to get a better look. She's used my name in every sentence tonight, which she does when she's feeling okay, and wants to reassure me that she knows who I am. She needs to wear her specs for this, and I anticipate a full-on hunt for them first. Instead, I notice that they're already on her head, perched in a nest of curls. Score one for Team Longville.

'We're making a kind of . . . history. A living history, of the people who live here. It's for my friend, Tom. The one who I told you about, who invented the flange bracket.'

'Oh yes,' she replies, popping on her glasses and peering at me over their tortoise-shell patterned frames. 'Tom. You like him, don't you?'

'Yes. I do,' I answer, wondering if we're about to wander into 'inappropriate conversation' territory. This happens occasionally, when she thinks I'm a female friend of the same age, or her younger sister. I'm an open-minded woman, but seriously, nobody wants to hear their mum's sexual conquest stories, do they?

'But do you *like* like him?' she asks, clearly trying to keep a straight face.

'Have you been watching the Disney Channel again?' I ask, staring at her through narrowed eyes as she grins at me.

She's developed a weird obsession with teen TV shows, like *The Suite Life of Zack and Cody* and *Good Luck Charlie*. She often sings the theme tunes, but always get them amusingly wrong – I will forever remember the time she changed the lyrics of a programme called *Jessie*, crooning along with her own words: 'Hey Jessie! There's a sausage sticking out of your face . . . Hey Jessie!' It was priceless.

'Might have been,' she replies defensively. 'Damn that Disney Channel. I know it's wrong, but it feels so good . . . anyway, I get the feeling that the inventor of the flange bracket is definitely more than a friend. Is he hot?'

I sigh, and lean back, my arms crossed over my chest.

'Mum, I'm not a fifteen-year-old cheerleader. And I barely know Tom – he's just a nice guy who gets nervous around new people, and I thought this might help him. He's a man who functions better with all the information.'

'Nobody ever has all the information,' she replies, quite accurately. 'He'll only have our version of the information. And I think you do like him.'

I chew my lips, and decide to ignore her. Partly because there's a tiny bit of me that suspects she's right, and that's a scary prospect. Budbury is full of attractive men, but I've just never responded to any of them in that way.

With Tom . . . well, I've noticed his attractiveness a little more than usual. I tell myself that it's simple biology – I've not had a boyfriend for well over three years. I suppose I was bound to crack at some point and give in to a little harmless window-shopping. But I need to keep it at that; between my jobs, my mum, and trying to save a bit of head-space for myself, there just isn't time for anything else.

Everything hangs together in such a fragile way already, throwing an affair into the mix would bring it all crashing down around me. It'd be like the last plastic bucket you attach to Buckaroo's back – just one item too many for a poor donkey (i.e. me) to bear.

'You can think what you want,' I reply, opening up a Word document. 'I can't stop your lurid fantasy life, Mum. But it's getting late now, and I'm going to crack on. Do you want to help?'

She glances through the window, and sees that it is dark. She follows that up with a look at the page-a-day calendar.

'Springtime,' she says. 'I love springtime. Every day, it'll stay light for a little bit longer . . . I always think that's magical. Okay. Let's get to work then! Just give me a minute to set the right atmosphere . . .'

She's big on atmospheres, my mum. We all grew up using aromatherapy oils, in a house scented by nature, often with weird sounds in the background. Other kids might have had *Now That's What I Call Music 1998*, but we had whale song, Gregorian chanting, and Ravi Shankar's greatest hits. I only remember the toned-down version of her – my older brothers and sister have more vivid recollections of living on the commune with her, when getting naked and painting yourself blue for a night round the campfire wasn't unusual.

Mum gets up, and lights a couple of candles. I recognise the smell as chamomile and jasmine. She puts a CD in – thankfully her collection of 'Music Inspired by the Ocean' rather than Ravi Shankar – and sits back down with me.

It's really nice, doing this together. It's been another busy day, and I've not had anywhere near enough time to relax. It's been sunny again, but I've mainly been in the van or indoors, at Briarwood and the café. Now I feel a bit like she's managed that 'bringing the outdoors in' trick that they talk about on home renovation shows.

It takes us a while – almost two hours and a couple of mugs of tea – but it's a fun two hours. I do the technical stuff, like the typing and saving and adding crazy fonts and colours and photos, and she adds her insights and comments.

I can tell as we do it that she doesn't always remember who all these people are straightaway – but after a few prompts, she gets up to speed, and has something to add. She's always been more instinct than fact anyway, which makes her a brilliant accomplice in this task.

By the time we've finished our masterwork, she's happy, smiling, and tired – in a good way. She casts a final eye over it and nods approvingly.

'It's very good,' she says, patting me on the shoulder.

'You should print it out and pin it to the wall. Just so, you know, you remember everyone.'

Of course. Because it's totally me who needs help on that front. You have to laugh sometimes.

'Great idea. I'll do that. Are you off to bed now?'

As she stands up and stretches – the usual signs – I'm not that surprised. It's after nine, which is a late night for us.

'Yes. Off to the land of cod for me, I think.' A quick wink there, to show the mistake was deliberate. 'Don't stay up too late, love – busy day tomorrow.'

I don't know if she has any real idea of what we're doing tomorrow, or works on the basis that it's always a busy day, but I nod and agree. I have a full shift at the café, and Katie and Saul are coming over to spend some time with Mum. She'll enjoy that, I know – the joy of having a toddler in the house is that there's always someone more confused than her. As her capabilities have been diminished over the last few years, along with at least some of her self-esteem, it does her good to be the 'grown-up' for a few hours.

I watch her pad silently down the hallway, still so lithe and graceful, and decide to throw caution to the wind – by brewing myself a wild and crazy peppermint tea. Five minutes of stillness, I tell myself; five minutes alone while I just let my mind relax and wander. Mainly it wanders right back to the Idiot's Guide to Budbury we've just produced, which makes me smile.

I sit, sipping at my mug, and feel a sense of complete

contentment wash over me. Quiet moments where I reflect on my friends and how lucky I am to have them. These are my people, and I love them – I just hope I've managed to capture them in all their glory for Tom.

I've built on the *Game of Thrones* riff from earlier, and laid it all out like one of those prologues from fantasy novels that seem to go on forever. I've added in some pictures and clip art – because I have the IT skills of a ten-year-old – but the content is what matters. It starts with Cherie, as all things in Budbury seem to, and covers all the key people he'll meet if he stays.

I attach some pictures – from Frank's horror-themed birthday party the summer before, and from our Budbury's Got Talent Christmas bash – and a little note wishing him happy reading. I press send before treating myself to one more read through:

The House of Moon-Farmer

Cherie Moon is the ultimate matriarch of Budbury. She's in her seventies, as tall as me, but much bigger and more solid. She's a former hippy rock-chick, and you can still see it: she has very long hair, which she often wears in a plait. She likes the occasional herbal cigarette, often walks around barefoot, and looks after everyone she meets. She owns the Comfort Food Café, the Rockery holiday cottages, and a few other places in the village – because despite being a hippy rock-chick, she's also a mini-mogul. She's generous, kind, and gives the best hugs. She will hug you

– don't even try and fight it. She also prides herself on figuring out people's comfort foods, and serving it to them in the café. Not everyone has one – but if you do, prepare to divulge it.

Cherie got married over a year ago to Frank. He's known as Farmer Frank, because he owns a huge farm, but in a cunning twist he's actually also called Frank Farmer. Cherie didn't take his name – and who can blame her, when hers is so pretty? Frank is eighty-one, and we have a big party for his birthday at the end of every summer season, the last weekend in August. He has silver hair and sparkly blue eyes and is as fit as his younger self ever was. His son and grandchildren live in Australia, and his first wife died a few years ago. His comfort food is burned bacon butties and strong tea, which Cherie provided for him every single day after he lost Bessy. From such humble beginnings grew a mighty romance. Frank has a wicked sense of humour, so prepare to take everything he says with a sackful of salt. Both Frank and Cherie are semi-retired, which gives them more time to sit in the café watching the world go by, and making fun of us all. Cherie used to live in her bachelorette pad above the café, but now lives on Frank's farm with him. The flat is still there, used intermittently by various strays in need of refuge.

The House of Hunter-Walker

Laura Walker's one of those strays, even though she never stayed in the flat above the café. Her husband David died in an accident, and she was a bit lost, struggling to cope even a few years later. So she got a job at the café for the summer, and came with her children Nate and Lizzie and their dog Jimbo (RIP). She was only supposed to stay until September, but stayed forever. She's really pretty and a bit plump, which annoys her so much she has to eat a piece of chocolate cake to cheer herself up. She has mad curly brown hair, is the owner of Midgebo, and lives in a cottage at the Rockery. Laura is sensitive, kind and a great believer in happy endings – she engineered all kinds of family reunions her first summer here, including getting Cherie back together with a sister she hadn't seen for decades. If Laura thinks you're less happy than you should be, she'll try and fix you. She manages the café, and is the world's best comfort food cook. She will experiment on you, so prepare to eat a lot of cake.

She lives in Hyacinth House with Lizzie, who is sixteen. She's blonde, wears a lot of black eyeliner, likes heavy metal music and is super cool. She goes out with Josh, of the House Jones. Nate is fourteen, also blonde, and is a typical boy – he plays a lot of football, guitar and video games, and thinks farting is a performance sport.

Matt Hunter also lives in the Rockery, in a big cottage called Black Rose. He is the local vet, and looks a bit like Han Solo – *Empire Strikes Back* era. He can be really quiet, and won't ever get in your face because he's quite a private person too. He is the master of comfortable silences, and prefers dogs to people. Apart from Laura – who is the love of his life, I reckon. The two of them have been together for a while now and I think it will stick. We're all hoping theirs will be the next big wedding.

The House of Brennan-Fletcher

Becca Fletcher is Laura's sister. She's in her thirties somewhere, and moved here from Manchester after a holiday romance with Sam. Becca is super-smart, acid-tongued, and totally deadpan. Possibly the most sarcastic person on the planet. She apparently used to be a bit of a wild child and got into a few bad situations, but these days she's all clean-living, apart from the fact that she's usually covered in baby vomit from Little Edie.

Little Edie was the outcome of Becca's romance with Sam Brennan, who is known as Surfer Sam, for reasons which become obvious when you see him. Sam is from Dublin, and grew up with about six thousand sisters. He's a coastal ranger and spends all his time outdoors. His comfort food is chicken and mushroom Pot Noodle, which reminds him of his childhood. He's funny and charming and before Becca, saw himself as something of a ladies' man. These days the main ladies in his life are Becca and Little Edie, who is six months old, and was actually born in the café. Seeing Little Edie born was both the most magical and most yuck experience of my life so far. They all live together in Sam's little terraced house in the centre of the village.

The House of Morgan-Harris-Hayes

This is a complicated one – a House of Many Names. I'll start with Zoe – Zoe Morgan. Zoe is very, very short, and very, very ginger. She's from Bristol, and is a bit like Becca in that she's spiky and sarky – but completely lovely underneath it. I don't think she had the easiest of childhoods, and things got worse when her best friend Kate Harris died of cancer. Kate had a sixteen-year-old daughter, Martha, and Zoe ended up becoming her guardian. It sounds like it was all going a bit pear-shaped, with Martha getting wilder and more self-destructive, so Zoe moved them down here to get away from all the bad influences. Zoe now runs the bookshop in the café.

Martha is seventeen now, and is the Queen of the Goths. She didn't settle in at first, but now she's best friends with Lizzie, and seems happy enough – although it's hard to tell with teenaged Goths. She has this weird, combative relationship with Zoe but you can tell they really love each other. Martha's comfort food is squashed up fish-finger sandwiches.

Cal Hayes is Martha's dad. She'd never even met him before she moved here – he had a fling with her mum in Thailand, and is from Australia. He runs Frank's farm for him, and looks a bit like Thor in the *Avenger* films. He's confident and capable and often wears a cowboy hat, but we won't hold that against him. He came here to see if he could help Martha stay on track, and him and Zoe ended up getting together. All three of them live in the village in the house where Ivy Wellkettle, our old pharmacist, used to live. Ivy moved up to Durham to be near her daughter while she does her medical training. The downside of this is that we don't have a pharmacy any more, but on the upside a nice home became available for the House of Morgan-Harris-Hayes.

The House of Jones
This one at least only has one surname – and one initial. They're known as the Scrumpy J Jones collective, and there are three of them: Joe, Joanne and Josh.

Joe runs the local Cider Cave, where he makes and sells artisan ciders – or at least he calls them 'artisan' now, since Lizzie, his son's girlfriend and teenage marketing guru, told him it sounds cool. The cave is popular with locals and tourists, and Joe is often to be heard clinking around the village with bags full of bottles. He's quiet, a bit grumpy, and considered a bit stingy – but when it counts, you can rely on Joe. His comfort food is home-made biscotti, which reminds him of visiting his gran in Italy as a kid. Joe has a really strong 'my luvver' Dorset accent – Frank sometimes speaks like that, as does Cherie, but Joe's is the thickest. Even I don't understand him sometimes.

His wife Joanne is a bit scary. She looks like something out of *Dallas* or *Dynasty*, with huge hair and perfect make-up. She runs a website called Rural Romance which hooks countryside types up for love and laughter – you should check it out!

Their son Josh is eighteen now. He's tall and lanky, always wears a beanie hat, and is a sweet kid who tries not to appear sweet.

The House of May
This is the last House – there are obviously others in Budbury, but I don't want to freak you out. It's also my favourite House.

The House of May consists of only one person – Edie May. Or Big Edie, as she now likes to be called, as there is a new Edie in town. She was thrilled when the baby came and was named after her, not least because she now gets to be Big – and bearing in mind she barely scrapes five feet when she's had her perm touched up, that's got to be a first.

Edie is ninety-one years old. In fact, she's ninety-two very soon – there'll be a party. You'll be forced to come. She lives on her own in a little terraced house in the village and is in amazing health for a woman her age. She tiny, and walks everywhere in her sensible shoes, often wearing a bright orange Vans backpack.

She used to be the village librarian, and is still really active on committees and things like that. She loves reading, chatting, and *Strictly Come Dancing*. Edie is an absolute joy and you'll love her – it's impossible not to. Don't make the mistake of dismissing her as nothing but a little old lady though; she's a very wise woman, and we've all turned to her on occasion. She's especially close to Becca, and also has lots of nieces and nephews and extended family who adore her.

The other thing you should know about Edie is that her fiancé died in the war back in the 1940s. Edie, though, doesn't seem to know that – she talks about him as though he's still alive, and usually takes extra food from the café back to her house for him. None of us ever challenge it – why would we? She's happy, she's healthy, and she still leads a really useful and fulfilling life.

The Budbury philosophy is a simple one: we accept people. Edie's probably the best example of that, but we all are to some extent – we're not the most conventional of communities. Something tells me you'll fit right in, Tom!

Chapter 8

'Can't you say something nice to each other, for just ten seconds? *Please?*'

Laura has her hands on her hips as she says this, her face screwed up in exasperation. It's the second day of the school holidays, and it feels as though it might be a long couple of weeks. Lizzie and Nate are bored, and that's never good.

Both teenagers momentarily pause in their exciting game of exchanging insults and throwing teaspoons at each other's faces, and appear to consider her request.

'Loser loser loser!' says Nate, bouncing a spoon off his sister's forehead with such force that it clatters onto the floor.

'Knob knob knob!' she screeches back, emptying the sugar bowl over his head.

Both of them dissolve into howls of laughter and give each other a high five – united at last. I'm not sure if that was quite Laura's plan, but at least they've stopped sniping. Nate shakes his head, and grains of brown sugar shimmer from his slightly-too-long blonde hair, landing on his shoulders like crystalline dandruff.

I see Laura's face torn between amusement and desperation and wonder yet again at the saintly powers you need to be a mother. She's tired, I can tell – she started early, getting ready for the breakfast shift, and worked all the way through to the post-lunch lull. It's been a lot busier than usual – school holidays – and the place looks a little the worse for wear. Kids have essentially been throwing spoons at each other and lobbing sugar around all day.

'I give up. You're awful children, and I'm going to divorce you both,' says Laura, throwing her hands into the air and turning to walk back into the kitchen. The kitchen looks a bit like a giant reached down, turned the whole building upside down, and shook it. There are only a few customers left now, so she starts the clean-up process.

I point at Lizzie and Nate, who are still laughing at their own hilarity.

'You two,' I say, as sternly as I can manage. 'Clean all that mess up. And while you're at it, make a start on the rest of the tables.'

'How much are we getting paid?' says Nate, who is becoming cheekier with every passing day.

'You're getting paid the gift of not getting a Doc Marten boot up your arse.'

They both ponder this, and then eventually he replies. ''Kay. Seems like a good deal.'

Both of them get up, and start to wander aimlessly

around the café, gathering dirty plates and napkins, working together to clear the tables. They're basically very good kids – they just need pointing in the right direction every now and then.

I glance through the windows and look longingly at the bay below. The Comfort Food Café is perched on the top of a cliff, surrounded by beautiful views of the beach and the hills around it.

It's another gorgeous spring day, and all the colours are vivid: golden sand, blue-green waves with frilly white toppers, the deep rust-red of the cliff faces, the shining emerald of their grassy tops. Even the people look like they've been created entirely out of primary colours: a child in a yellow cagoule, a mum with hair the same shade, a group of walkers on a distant hill path clad head to toe in bright blue.

I'd love to be out there, feeling the breeze on my face and the salt on my skin. I don't seem to have a lot of time for that kind of thing these days, and I miss it.

'You all right, my love?' says Cherie, approaching from behind. Her voice startles me, and I snap back into the present. I turn around to face her, and can't help but smile. Her long hair is slung over her shoulder in a fat plait, and she's wearing an apron that has Wonder Woman's body on it. The original Wonder Woman, of course.

She's holding out a plate bearing cake – the leftover coffee and walnut that Laura baked this morning – and gesturing to the table. One of the many wonderful things about working here is the food, and the fact that at least once a day, no matter how busy we are, Cherie insists that we sit down and have a chat.

I brush stray sugar off the seat, and plonk myself down on it. As soon as I do, that thing happens – that thing where you don't realise how tired you are until you stop for a second, and the exhaustion sneaks in and bops you over the head like an inflatable cartoon mallet.

I see Laura asking the remaining customers if they need anything else, offering coffee top-ups, and pausing to tell the kids to carry on working. They pull tongues at her behind her back, and she immediately says – without even looking – 'Put them back in. You'll need them for being rude to me later.' Mum powers to the max.

She wipes her hands down on her pinny, and tucks one of her many wild curls behind her ear as she sits. She's brought the coffee pot, which can only be a good thing. The coffee pot is my friend.

'Phew! What a day!' she says, blowing air out of her cheeks and kicking off her Skechers. 'But at least it means the time passed quickly . . . you all right, Willow?'

She's the second person to ask me that in as many minutes, so I start to wonder if I've accidentally lipsticked my eyes or forgotten to put clothes on.

'I am indeed all right,' I reply, once I do a quick check to ensure neither of those things are true. 'And even better now I have coffee and cake.'

I see Laura and Cherie exchange glances, so I stuff a

huge spoonful of cake into my mouth in anticipation. They'll be talking for the next few minutes, I can tell.

'You've seemed a bit distracted today,' says Laura, tactfully. I frown, wondering what she's talking about.

'You put the butter in the freezer instead of the fridge, the milk in the oven, and the avocado salad in the blender.'

'Oh. I made an avocado salad smoothie?'

'You did. I'm actually thinking I might put it on the menu, but . . . well, are you *actually* all right? You're tense. You're never tense. Ever. In all the time I've known you, I've not seen you tense.'

I lay down my spoon, sip some coffee, and wait. Cherie soon pipes up: 'She's right. You're never tense. Even when you've had a bad day with your mum, you're just tired, and sad, and pink. What's going on?'

She lays her hand on my arm as she speaks, and I fight away a slight sense of being invaded. These are my friends. My allies in life. My cheerleaders. They're worried about me, and that is good – we all need someone to worry about us every now and then.

'Sorry, ladies,' I say, trying to smile reassuringly. 'Bit of a headache, that's all.'

'I noticed that lump on the side of your head . . .' replies Laura, whipping a hankie out of her apron pocket and looking dangerously like she might be about to spit on it and attack me.

'Yeah. Let's just say I walked into a frying pan and leave it at that,' I say, leaning out of reach.

Cherie nods, and drops the subject – but not before I see the look of pity and understanding flit across her weathered face.

'Plus,' I add, hoping to distract them both from feeling sorry for me, 'I have a friend visiting in . . . well, very soon, hopefully. If he bothers coming, anyway.'

Both women immediately perk up. Laura's eyebrows shoot so far up her face that they disappear behind her hair, and Cherie actually whistles out loud. Wow. I must be a tragic figure indeed, if referring to a friend has this effect. I really should get out more.

'And if . . .' I add, unable to resist. 'He's actually real. I mean, I could have imagined him. It's always possible. I might have accidentally created an imaginary friend, along with an avocado salad smoothie.'

Cherie nods sagely, accepting what I say as an entirely feasible proposition. What can I say? She's known me for a long time.

'If,' she says, gazing past me thoughtfully, 'you were going to create an imaginary friend, I can just picture him. Tall, dark, handsome.'

'Yes,' adds Laura, totally deadpan. 'Tall, dark, handsome. Wearing an old-school *Star Wars* T-shirt, and accompanied by a bloody big dog.'

I'm momentarily lost for words, speechless at their powers of perception, until Laura bursts out laughing and spoils the illusion. They're looking right over my shoulder at the doors that lead into the garden where, I see as soon as I twist my head around, Tom and Rick Grimes are currently lurking.

Tom is moving hesitantly from one foot to another, looking behind him as though he's considering making a run for it. Rick Grimes is muzzled, but still looks happier than his owner.

I leap out of my chair so fast it topples over, and make a mad dash for the door, leaving Cherie and Laura in my dust. That'll give 'em something to talk about.

I emerge into the garden just as Tom has clearly decided to leave. He's started to make his way back to the pathway that leads back down the hill.

'Oi! You! The man with the dog!' I yell, just as he reaches the wrought-iron archway that marks the entrance to the Comfort Food Café. It's decorated with metallic roses as well as the name of the place, and most people find it charming. Tom is obviously not one of them.

'Freeze!' I shout. 'We have you surrounded!'

He does indeed freeze, but when he turns around, he has a sheepish grin on his face. It's a good grin – a bit lopsided, like he can't quite keep it straight.

'Caught in the act . . .' he says, as I trot over towards him. Rick Grimes gets excited as soon as he sees me, his muzzled head bouncing up and down and making him look like Hannibal Lecter trying to reach his fava beans. I'm not foolish enough to think for a minute that it's me he's interested in – he just associates me with Bella, his One True Love. He's going to be disappointed though, because she's at home today. I lean down anyway, and tickle him behind his velvety ears, running my hands through the thicker fur on his neck.

I stand up straight again as soon as dog greetings are dispensed with, and see Tom taking in the café garden. It's a higgledy-piggledy place, wooden benches and tables placed on uneven ground, parasols flapping in the sea breeze, napkins swirling. It's been busy out here today, and it's littered with empty plates and mugs and juice glasses. The perfect next job for Lizzie and Nate.

'This is nice,' says Tom, his eyes doing a full circuit of the ramshackle structure of the café, the new bookshop in the extension off to the side, and breathtaking views of the bay. 'Like the café on the edge of the world.'

'Yep. I know what you mean. It'd be a good place to hunker down for the zombie apocalypse.'

He narrows his eyes and I can tell that he's giving this issue some serious thought, as I also have, on quieter days.

'Plenty of food and water . . . cliffs on one side . . . steep hill on the other . . .' he says, glancing at the pathway.

'We could get that fence reinforced,' I say, joining him in his zombie-check. 'Put some spikes on it to catch them as they pass.'

'Good idea – but a perimeter fence at the bottom would be good as well. How are you for drugs?'

'Well, Cherie's flat probably has some old spliffs in it, but beyond that . . . hmm. Maybe we'd need to raid a pharmacy beforehand? Stock up on antibiotics and first aid supplies?'

'Definitely. Antibiotics are the new currency in the post-zombie apocalypse world. Personnel, weapons?'

'Weapons . . . well, a lot of knives. Some wicked-looking blenders. One of those moon-shaped cutting devices that Laura uses to shred herbs. Frank probably has a couple of shotguns as well. Personnel would be good, if we get the full crew to safety – we have farmers for the long-term sustainability plan, we have cowboys who can probably wrestle crocs; we have a vet – which is as good as a doctor in desperate times – and we have an abundance of street fighters. Plus – you'll like this – the café has its own back-up generator, and that shed over there houses a massive gas barbecue and canisters.'

'Okay,' he says, dragging his eyes away from the shed and giving me a big smile, 'I'd say we're sorted then. Bring it on!'

We simultaneously look off down the path again, and I know we've both convinced ourselves that the walking dead will be slowly staggering up towards us at any moment, with their tattered clothing and clumped-up hair. When it doesn't happen, I say: 'Well. I'm glad we cleared that up. Now come and do something I think you'll find much more frightening – meet Cherie and Laura.'

'I think I can see them,' he says quietly. 'They've practically got their face squashed up against the glass, watching us. And I can tell which one is which because of the handy fact-file you sent over. Okay . . . let's do this. Where shall I put Rick?'

'There aren't any other dogs in there, so he'll be fine. Don't let him near the kitchen, though – he might end up eating his own body weight in chocolate chips.'

I turn and head back to the café, not giving him the chance to come up with any more excuses. Cherie and Laura immediately leap into action, scurrying around clearing tables and pretending that they haven't spent the last few minutes staring at us.

I open the doors, and see Tom pause as we walk through. Sometimes I forget how weird this place must look to fresh eyes. Cherie has owned the café for a long time, and the interior design is as quirky as she is.

The tables and chairs are covered in gingham cloths and decorated with little vases full of wildflowers. There's a long wooden counter and a chiller cabinet, packed with home-made cakes, fresh sandwiches, pies, and little individual jugs of rich cream. So far, so normal, for a café.

What sets it apart is the fact that literally every available space is crammed with random objects that Cherie has collected over the years. You know when you go into some chain restaurant, and you can tell that there's a corporate design – fake antique books, pretend old photos, plastic sea shells, that kind of thing?

Well the Comfort Food Café is the direct opposite of that. There are all kinds of objects hanging from the ceiling – oars from a rowing boat, mobiles made of old vinyl singles, conch shells, a witch's broomstick, dangling fishing nets, a miniature cider press. The shelves that line the walls are like something from an eccentric flea market. A quick glance shows an old black-and-gold Singer sewing machine, half a kayak, framed pictures of the coast taken by Cherie's late first husband, and piles of old-school board games like KerPlunk and Chinese Chequers.

There's an entire corner full of books – now neatly categorised by Zoe, our resident bookworm – and colouring pads and pens and puzzles for kids. The whole effect is a treat for the eyes, and a minimalist's living nightmare. Tom is cataloguing it all, and I see that it's making him smile. It might be the opposite of the way he runs his own home, but I'm glad he likes it.

'Yeah, I know,' I say, as I lead him through the door. 'It's a lot. Watch your head, you might get whacked by a low-flying kipper.'

Laura bustles over, wiping her hands on a tea towel, pretending badly that she's only just noticed us. And the Oscar most definitely doesn't go to . . .

'Hello!' she says, beaming, tilting her head so she can look up at him. Tom is maybe a full foot taller than Laura, and the effect is comical. 'I'm Laura! It's so nice to meet you – can I get you some cake? Coffee and walnut? Or I have some sticky chocolate and orange pudding left? Or a fresh scone and some cherry jam?'

Poor Tom looks thoroughly overwhelmed – whether at the company or the bewildering choice of baked goods, I don't know. Luckily, he's given a bit of breathing space by the fact that the last remaining official customers make their way out of the café, waving as they go. I hear one of them make a comment about how he's so full now, he'll have to roll all the way down the hill. Job done, Team Comfort Food.

'He looks like he needs the pudding to me,' says Cherie, ambling over towards us. She raises her eyebrows, and he nods, smiling.

'Pudding it is! With butterscotch sauce!' replies Laura, clapping her hands together with glee. She never feels better than when she's plying someone with cake. She's like the Walter White of sugar.

Cherie is absently-minded stroking Rick Grimes's head, and I realise she's waiting for an introduction. Dang it. Distracted again.

'Cherie, this is Tom. Tom, this is Cherie.'

'Of the House Moon-Farmer,' he responds, correctly.

'You can explain that one later,' she says, looking understandably confused. 'But for now, who is this beautiful big boy?'

'I've just told you . . . it's Tom,' I reply, in a 'duh' tone of voice. Cherie bites her lip as she tries not to laugh, and Tom gently adds, 'I think she means the dog.'

I can feel myself blushing, and I don't think I've blushed since I was thirteen – our mother always raised us not to be embarrassed, and to own everything we did with the courage of our convictions. I applaud the sentiment, but it's no use to me now.

Tom quickly covers for me. 'This is Rick Grimes. He loves people, but isn't too keen on other dogs. Apart from Bella, that is.'

'Ah, well – that's understandable. Bella's milkshake brings all the boys to the yard,' says Cherie, bizarrely quoting Kelis. 'But there are no other pooches here now, so let's unleash the beast, shall we?'

Tom nods, and unfastens the muzzle. Rick's big teddy bear face emerges in all its glory, and he proceeds to lick all our hands in gratitude.

'Pudding! Custard! Coffee!' shouts Laura like a demented tea-lady dictator, and gestures us all towards one of the bigger tables. As is traditional, she doesn't say a word until Tom has tasted his cake, waiting for his reaction.

His face melts into something orgasmic at the first spoonful, and she grins at him.

'Plenty more where that came from,' she says, patting his hand. 'So, Tom – how do you know Willow?' I suspect she knows the answer to this question already, but wants to hear his version.

'Umm,' he begins, licking his lips clean. 'We met at Briarwood. I've . . . well, I've just bought it.'

Cherie is immediately enraptured, and proceeds to question him about all the details – why he bought it, what he plans to do with it, if he's staying, where he's living, if he needs any help, what the timescales are, whether he wears boxers or briefs. He answers everything apart from the last one, because she didn't actually ask that, I made it up. He answers, but is looking increasingly flustered by the end of the interrogation.

'One more question,' she says, finally running out of steam. Tom looks like he might be about to face-plant in his pudding at the prospect. 'Do you want some more coffee?'

He nods in relief, and she's in the middle of pouring it when Lizzie and Nate wander over to us. They've been watching from the other side of the counter, feigning non-interest. I'd been wondering how long it'd take them to give in and join the grown-ups.

I introduce them, and Nate immediately says, 'Cool T-shirt.'

'Thanks,' replies Tom, looking down at his own chest. 'I suppose you're more of a *Force Awakens* kind of guy, as you weren't even born when this one came out?'

'I am,' Nate responds, glancing at his mum. 'But we're not allowed to mention it in maternal company.'

We all look at Laura, who visibly shudders.

'They killed Han Solo,' she says sadly. 'I shall never recover.'

Lizzie pulls a face – the kind of face that only teenaged girls can manage in response to their own mother's embarrassing behaviour. 'We're off down to the beach. Sam's doing one of his utterly fascinating talks on ammonites, and we promised we'd help out. Tom . . . can I take your photo? It's for my online journal.'

Lizzie, since she first arrived here in Budbury, has been

the village's unofficial documentarian. Our whole lives are captured on her Instagram account, and one day, it'll probably form the basis for a historical archive, leading future generations to believe that it's completely normal to live your entire life in fancy dress and eat nothing but cake.

Tom looks horrified, but slowly nods his head. He poses awkwardly, glancing at me just as she takes the picture.

'Don't worry,' I say, reassuringly. 'We've all been there. It's part of life in House Walker-Hunter.'

Lizzie frowns, not having a clue what I'm talking about, but decides she doesn't really care. As she and Nate trot off towards the garden, I can already see her fingers flying across the keyboard of her phone, and know that within minutes Tom's image will be circulated to the relevant parties more efficiently than the FBI's Most Wanted list.

She looks over her shoulder, and gives me a cheeky thumbs up paired with an exaggerated wink. Lord help us all – I do believe I'm being given romantic encouragement by a sixteen-year-old.

'I think,' says Cherie, her sandalled feet now trapped beneath Rick Grimes's hefty body, 'that you need to explain all this "house" stuff to us, Willow. Just wait a minute, though, here comes Zoe . . . her house must have loads of names!'

Zoe comes flying into the room, a bundle of fizzing energy and crazy ginger hair. Her eyes immediately latch onto Tom, and I know instinctively that she's already seen

Lizzie's post and dashed straight across to see what all the fuss is about.

'Hello!' she says, pulling up a chair and helping herself to a coffee. 'Heard we had a visitor . . . rush hour at the shop seems to be over with, so I thought I'd have a break.'

'I'm Zoe,' she says directly to Tom. 'I run Comfort Reads, next door. How's the interrogation going? Has Cherie held you down and shone a torch in your eyes yet?'

Cherie pretends to look offended, but really has no defence. Tom looks like a rabbit trapped in the headlights in the face of all this attention, but manages to reply. 'No, but I was worried in case she tried to wrench my fingernails off at one stage . . .'

'I get it,' says Zoe, knowingly. 'I only arrived here in September last year, and within minutes they knew more about me than I did. Literally. But . . . well, just grin and bear it, Tom. The pros outweigh the cons – I'm still here, anyway.'

'Running the bookshop?'

'Yep. It's good. I get to sell a few books, read a few books. Maybe one day I'll even write a book, who knows?'

'You could!' chips in Laura, sounding excited at the prospect. 'You could set it in a little café by the beach, and make it all about the wacky-yet-lovable characters who live here . . .'

Zoe rolls her eyes, and steals a piece of Laura's scone.

'Not my scene,' she answers. 'More likely to make it about a serial killer who hides out at the llama farm and kills us all in our sleep. But hey, that's just me. So, Tom, how are you settling in? And have you remembered all our names? Took me days . . .'

He glances at me to check it's okay to spill the beans. 'That's what this "house" business is all about,' he says. 'It was Willow's way of helping me settle in. She did me a fact-file on all of you.'

'Did she now?' replies Cherie, looking at me through narrowed eyes. It's her 'one tough mama' look, but it doesn't intimidate me in the slightest. She's about as tough as Blu Tack once you get past the Amazonian appearance.

I give her a no-big-deal shrug and say, 'It was the only way I was going to get him out of his pit of solitude. Really, you should be thanking me – without my intervention, you'd never have found out anything about the man who bought Briarwood.'

'Yes I would, my love,' she replies, grinning. 'You should know me better than that. If all else failed, I'd have just ordered a drone flight over the house, wouldn't I? Or sent Lizzie up there with a long-angle lens. So . . . what was in this fact-file, then, Tom? All our dirty secrets, was it?'

'Nope,' he says simply. 'Just the facts, ma'am. Plus a load of Willow's views about how wonderful you all are. It's sweet, actually.'

'We should get a copy printed off,' adds Laura straight-away. 'Get it framed and put it up in the café. Or give it to Zoe so she can turn it into a best-selling bonk-buster about sex and secrets on the Jurassic coast . . .'

Zoe snorts with laughter, which wakes up Rick Grimes and possibly people in the next county.

'That could work,' she says, obviously giving it some thought. 'It might be worth doing just to completely and utterly embarrass the kids. Can you imagine? Nate and Lizzie and Martha reading lurid sex scenes about bodices getting ripped off?'

'I've never had my bodice ripped off . . .' replies Laura, looking slightly sad about that fact.

'Don't worry, love,' says Cherie, giving her a nudge. 'I'll have a word with Matt next time I see him. I'm sure he'd be happy to oblige. Anyway . . . did you include yourself in this here fact-file, young Willow? Was there a chapter on House Longville, or was it just us lot?'

Chapter 9

She has a point, so I keep myself busy by eating yet more cake. It's a good job I inherited my mother's metabolism or I'd be waddling around like a sumo wrestler.

I hadn't included a section on House Longville, no. Partly because Tom already knew me – kind of. In fact, if I was being pedantic, I could claim to have known him since I was eight – even if our conversation was limited to one huge scream and me slamming the door in his face.

But partly, I simply didn't want to lie – and a section on House Longville wouldn't have been complete without reference to the reality of my mum's condition, and my glamorous life. Maybe I just didn't want to face up to it all myself, who knows? If I made myself sit down and really, truly think about everything, I'd probably end up miserable instead of just tired.

Tom, though, is now looking at me with interest – as though he was wondering the same as Cherie, and trying to piece together *my* fact-file.

'She didn't include that, no,' he says, smiling gently.

'Maybe you ladies can fill me in on everything related to Willow.'

'Be kind,' I add quickly. 'Or I'll curse you with my ancient Romany blood.'

'You don't have ancient Romany blood,' replies Cherie.

'Or *do* I?' I ask, making my voice ominous, waving my hands and making woo-woo-woo sound effects to give it more mystery.

'Okay – I'll start!' pipes up Laura, who has clearly decided this will be a good opportunity to find out more. 'She's called Willow Cassandra Longville, and she's 26. She has . . . um, three brothers and sisters?'

I nod, to show that she's on track so far.

'Oh no! I don't actually know their names . . .'

'I do,' says Zoe, holding up her hand like she's in school. 'Willow's mum named them all after their characteristics when they were born. So there's Willow, who was long and lean; Auburn, who – like all God's best children – has red hair; Van, who had a funny ear; and Angel – who looked like a little blonde cherub. Ten points for me. I don't know where any of them are though . . .'

All four of them are looking at me now, as though waiting for an explanation. Abridged version ahoy.

'Neither do I, really. Van, I think, is living in Tibet some-where, halfway up a mountain in a Buddhist community. Auburn, last time I heard, was living on a cannabis farm in Peru, although that might have changed. Maybe she's upgraded to a cocaine farm in Columbia. Angel . . . well, he's the black sheep of the family. He changed his name to Andrew, and he's a biology teacher in Aberdeen. I haven't seen any of them for quite a long time.'

Tom is looking fascinated – or maybe just relieved that someone else has been thrust into the spotlight – but Laura is looking thoughtful. Like she's turning this new information over in her mind, and she's not altogether pleased with the picture it's painting.

'But why?' she asks eventually, frowning. 'Wouldn't it be . . . helpful for you, if you weren't doing everything on your own?'

Everyone else here knows, of course, about my mum. Everyone apart from Tom – and it's probably about time I told him. I don't know why I've avoided it. I think maybe I was enjoying spending time with someone who just saw me as Willow – not poor-love-she-has-such-a-lot-to-deal-with-Willow. But if he's going to stay, he'll need to know – just in case she turns up at Briarwood and puts him in plank position.

I turn to face him, and say: 'My mum has Alzheimer's. She doesn't actually look that different from when you used to know her, but she is different. Sometimes. Sometimes she's the same. What can I say? It keeps life interesting.'

I'm pretending it's not a big deal, which isn't like me at all. I don't usually pretend anything. I'm feeling nervous and jittery, and wondering how Tom will react. It shouldn't matter – but for some reason, it does. I'm staring at the coffee pot, because it's much easier than meeting anybody's eyes right now.

'I'm really sorry,' Tom says quietly. He reaches out, and touches my hand gently beneath the table. My fingers find themselves tangled in his, and I'm horrified to realise that my eyes have sneakily filled with tears.

I'm very confused by all of this. I might not have my family with me, but I am surrounded by wonderful friends who offer me all the support I could ever ask for. I've never been aware of feeling alone or isolated – but somehow, the touch of Tom's strong hand on mine tells me I have been. It's overwhelming, and I don't know quite how to react.

I'm aware of the silence that's fallen over the table, and that adds to the sense of weirdness. These women are so rarely silent – they're always laughing and joking and sharing stories and winding each other up. Now, though, they're all quiet, and I don't need to look up to know that Laura and Cherie will also have tears in their eyes. Zoe won't. She's made of sterner stuff, at least on the outside.

I'm clinging onto Tom's fingers, blinking away the annoying liquid pooling beneath my eyelids, and waiting for the inevitable moment when Cherie dives in to hug me to within an inch of my life, or Laura force-feeds me carrot cake. Rick Grimes, as though sensing the tension, rests his big teddy bear head on my knees and looks up at me with plaintive brown eyes.

Just as it's becoming unbearable, and I fear I may have

to start a tap-dancing routine along the counter to lighten the mood, the doors to the café swing open.

We all swivel around to look; with perfect timing, my mother has arrived. I take in her outfit, and I don't know whether to laugh or cry – but as I'm already crying, I go with that to save time.

She's wearing a bright red sweatshirt and black leggings. Over the leggings, she's added a pair of equally bright red knickers. At first, I think she's had a wardrobe malfunction – I lay her clothes out in order, to help her get dressed herself in the morning, but today it looks like she got the order mixed up and added pants after leggings. These things happen to the best of us.

It's only when I notice the tea towel draped from her shoulders that I start to worry – that's a new one.

Within seconds, she's followed through the door by a harassed-looking Katie, and Saul. Saul, I see, is dressed exactly the same as my mum – he has tight pyjama trousers on, red pants over the top, and a tea towel wrapped around his little shoulders. I realise that it's not actually a wardrobe malfunction at all – it's deliberate, and they're both dressed as superheroes. Both of them raise their arms into the air, and mock-fly into the room in the style of the man from Krypton.

They swoop and whoosh around the café, dodging tables and jumping over imaginary obstacles, completely and utterly happy with their game. We all watch, and you have to smile – they're having so much fun, it's infectious.

Katie, who walks timidly up to the table, looks as though she's having a bit less fun. Katie is small, quiet, and shy, with dark blonde hair and a voice you sometimes struggle to hear. She's probably lost it from all the time she spends saying 'No, Saul – don't do that!' He's a bit of a handful, and getting more so now he's so mobile. Little boys have as much energy as a hurricane, and can be just as destructive, I've noticed.

'I'm sorry,' she says to me, shaking her head. 'She just really wanted to get out and about. I tried to distract her at home, but you know how agitated she can get when she sets her mind on something – I didn't want to make it worse.'

'It's absolutely fine,' I say, finally pulling my hand away from Tom's – it seems to have accidentally stayed there – and standing up to talk to Katie. I know she won't pull up a chair and join us. She's still on the periphery of life here, and seems grateful yet guarded when she's on the receiving end of the café's community spirit.

'Seriously,' I add, when she looks unconvinced, 'I'm not exactly slaving away, am I? I'm stuffing my face with cake and talking to my friends. And you did the right thing – if you'd tried to stop her, she'd have got more and more upset, and then I'd have had a really unsettled night with her. How's it been today, anyway?'

'Oh . . . good, really. She took her meds without any problems, and watched some old episodes of *Wizards of Waverly Place*.'

'I like that one . . .' I say, smiling. I refuse to be ashamed.

'Me too!' she confesses, hiding a giggle with her hands. 'Then she did some gardening with Saul, they both enjoyed that. Scrambled eggs for lunch. And then . . . well, they turned into Superman, and decided they wanted to fly all the way here. Actually they asked for Metropolis, but there isn't one of those within flying distance, so we decided the café would be a good second choice.'

'It's fine – really, it is,' I say, as she's still looking a bit sheepish. 'How's she been with . . . reality? Our version of it, at least.'

'In and out. She remembered my name, but she thinks Saul is Angel today. It doesn't do any harm – he's used to being called a little devil more than an angel, so I think he quite likes it. They're quite a tag team, those two.'

Laura has stood up and started clearing the table, and Zoe is making noises about heading back to the bookshop. Cherie's watching my mum and Saul fly around the room, smiling at their antics, arms folded contentedly over her ample bosom. One of Cherie's greatest skills is her ability to go with the flow, and see the funny side of pretty much everything.

My mum notices Zoe, and waves to her, flapping her tea towel cape as she does.

'See you later, Auburn!' she shouts. Zoe gives her a little salute, and leaves.

The party is breaking up now. Everyone heads off apart from my mum, Saul, and Rick Grimes, who is merrily running around the room with them, knocking over chairs and crashing into the table legs and letting out the occasional excited woof.

Tom calls him over, and for a minute the dog pauses, and gives him such a funny look – the kind kids give their parents when they tell them it's time to leave the ball pool. His ears droop in disappointment, and he trots back to Tom's side, panting after his exertions.

'I have an idea,' says Cherie, stretching her arms over her head. She's so tall, her fingertips collide with the starfish mobile above her head. 'Why don't you and Tom take Rick for a proper walk, and Lynnie can stay here with us? She seems happy enough – and if that changes, we can ask her for a yoga lesson. You know she'll stay for that. I can run her home to you in an hour or so, and bring some leftovers for your dinner. What do you say?'

Laura is hovering in the background listening, and I know that inside she'll be plotting mini-breaks to Paris and romantic dinners for two. Nothing will have gone unnoticed, and they'll be concocting a fairytale happy-ever-after ending for me and Tom by now. I understand that – and they were definitely right when it came to Becca and Sam, and Zoe and Cal.

But my life isn't the stuff of fairytales. The curse can't be broken with a kiss from a handsome prince, and I'm not going to wake up one day and find that my mother has miraculously been healed. There will be no magical apples, or fairy godmothers, or sumptuous balls in a pastel-coloured castle. And if someone came along with a glass Doc Marten boot, I wouldn't even try it on. This is the way of things, and that's okay – dreaming of more will only lead to tears before bedtime.

I'm about to say no, and find an excuse to leave with Supermum in tow, when Tom grabs hold of my hand and tugs me towards the door.

'Great idea!' he shouts to Cherie. 'Thank you!'

I tear my hand from his and stand still with my hands on my hips, glaring up at him.

'Don't argue – Rick needs a walk. You need a break. And we can carry on making zombie apocalypse plans.'

'I wasn't going to argue,' I reply, poking him in the chest with one finger. 'I was going to get my bag. My phone's in my bag, and you know that people who go out without their phones always suffer when society crumbles, don't you?'

'Oh. Right. Okay then . . .'

I give him a 'you pillock' look, and go behind the counter to get my stuff and hang up my glamorous work overall. I might not get a fairy-tale ending but right here, and right now, I can at least enjoy a walk in the fresh air on a beautiful day.

I glance back at my mum. Cherie has her settled with Saul, both of them drinking cranberry juice through a twisty straw. She lifts her gaze to mine, and gives me a sweet little smile and a tiny wave of her fingers. I don't know if she understands what's happening, or who I am

– she definitely thought Zoe was Auburn, as she often does – but she seems content. Content and safe, which is good enough for me.

Just as I'm about to leave, I see her mouth two words at me. I screw my face up in confusion, unable to make them out. She tries again, but I hold my hands up to show I still don't get it.

She sighs and puts her glass down, clearly exasperated at my lack of lip-reading ability. Then she yells, at the top of her voice: 'Flange bracket!'

Chapter 10

At first, I'm thinking we'll head down to the beach, but I can tell from Tom's face that he's nervous. It's a lovely day in the school holidays, so the place is packed with kids and dogs and picnics. I know Rick Grimes loves people, but he might go all killer on the pooches. And I've seen first-hand what damage certain dogs – i.e. Laura's black Labrador Midgebo – can do to unsuspecting picnics. It's not pretty.

Instead, I suggest we go back to the cottage, where Rick can adore Bella and we can all relax. It's not an especially long walk, about fifteen minutes, but it is very pretty. Part of it is across the coastal pathway, the sea shimmering beneath us like a blue-green bed sheet, and the rest is through Frank's farm. The fields are lush and green, some planted with crops, others hosting big herds of black-and-white mooing cows.

We actually bump into Frank and Cal on the way, but they're doing something important with a tractor, so we don't stop for long. Just long enough for Tom to break the ice and tick two more people off his Budbury hit list, and for Frank to tell me casually that he 'lent my mother a pair of skivvies' this morning. Best not to think about that one too hard.

It's a lovely stroll, the sun warming my skin, the birdsong lifting my spirits, and the exercise helping to work off all that cake. I clamp down on a teeny, tiny part of me that feels guilty about this – about abandoning my mum and recklessly running off into the distance with a strange man and a dog that looks like a teddy bear.

I clamp down on it because I know I don't have anything to feel guilty about. She's happy enough, and I am a human being too. I exist, even though it sometimes doesn't feel like there's enough of me to go around. Besides, she'd be horrified at the thought of me seeing her like that – like a burden.

Rick starts to get excited as soon as we reach the pathway that leads up to the cottage, and I tell Tom to let him off the lead. I see Bella peeking through the window watching us approach, but by the time we make it inside, she's curled up on her dog bed. Rick gallops over and starts nuzzling her, his fat tail thumping on the parquet.

'Shall we sit in the garden?' I ask, as Tom wanders around the kitchen staring at random things. Pictures on the walls, Mum's collection of weird CDs, the potted plants in the windowsill, the big-print calendar. He runs his fingers casually over the scarred wooden surface of the table, as though he's never encountered such a thing before, a look of fascination on his face.

'Willow calling Tom,' I say, in a static-radio voice. 'Willow calling Tom, over! Do you copy, over?'

He looks up, surprised, and grins.

'Sorry!' he replies, snatching his fingers away. 'You caught me fondling wood this time. It's lovely in here. Exactly like I'd imagine a slightly bonkers family home to be. I was just imagining little Willow, growing up here, surrounded by all this stuff, and all those brothers and sisters.'

I pull a face and reply: 'It smells better now. Teenaged boys are stink-pits. And it wasn't perfect, but yeah – it was my place. I've never lived anywhere else, apart from a brief and failed stint at going away to college . . . Anyway. Garden?'

He nods, and I grab a jug of fresh orange juice from the fridge. I think we've probably both had enough coffee and cake for one day. I open the kitchen window, and dock my phone on the speakers – on the very rare occasions when I'm here without my mother, it's nice to listen to music that I enjoy, rather than her bohemian mama sound machine.

I press play, and turn the volume up so it will carry out into the garden. I feel good immediately. It's one of those songs that just makes me smile.

'Girls Aloud?' he says, raising his eyebrows at me. 'Really? Thought you'd be more of an indie girl . . .'

'Girls Aloud,' I say, carrying our glasses and juice outside, 'are one of the most under-rated pop acts of all time. I mean, just listen. It's brilliant, isn't it?'

'Sound of the Underground' is booming away, and I can't help but bop along as I go. I mean, I think you'd have to be technically dead to not bop along to 'Sound of the Underground', and even then, there might be a little toe-tapping to that surfing bit.

I put the drinks down on the table, and let myself have a few moments of sheer, uninhibited dance-related joy. I shimmy vigorously around Wurzel, and jump across the rows of carrots in the vegetable patch, and clap my hands, and stamp my Docs until I'm all puffed out. It's like I'm possessed by a dance demon – I literally can't stop until the song does. Damn those girls and their fiendishly catchy tunes.

I flop down on the bench next to Tom, blowing hair out of my eyes and grinning, my slightly wobbly legs spread out in front of me.

'Phew!' I wipe my forehead with the back of my hand. 'I feel better for that. You should've joined in.'

Tom is looking at me with amazement. Huh. Weird. It's almost as though he's never seen a giant woman with neon pink hair getting jiggy with a scarecrow before. He must have led a sheltered life.

'I'm not quite that far along on my journey to loosening up,' he says, shaking his head and smiling. 'And besides, I didn't want to ruin the moment. It was like a comedy version of that scene in *Flashdance* – you know, where she leaps around with a welding torch?'

'Oh yes. I know the one. Always thought that looked

really dangerous. I like a good dance, what can I say? Anyway . . . have you seen Wurzel?'

The scarecrow is dressed up as a superhero as well, with a bath towel hanging off his scrawny stick shoulders, a cardboard eye mask, and yes, a pair of Frank's old-man knickers. All becomes clear.

'I have. He looks cool. So – I'm guessing you grew up in a world where the phrase "dance like nobody's watching" was a way of life?'

'I suppose. There were so many of us, you couldn't do anything without somebody watching. It's just the way our lives were – communal, whether we liked it or not. I'm guessing your childhood was a bit . . . different?'

I sip my juice, and cast a quick glance at him. This corner of the garden is in shade, but the rest is still bathed in sunlight. If you look really quickly from one bit to the other, it makes your eyes go weird and gives you a bit of a head rush. Take your thrills where you find them, boys and girls.

He shifts a bit next to me, and I feel his leg brush against mine. Not that he's noticed – he seems pretty lost in thought.

'You don't have to talk about it if you don't want to,' I add, nudging him. 'This is a low-pressure environment, I promise. We can just listen to Girls Aloud if you like. Maybe slip in some Sugababes after.'

'No, it's okay, I don't mind. I'm just . . . not used to talking about it, I suppose. Well. My childhood was definitely very different than yours, even when my parents were alive. They were both really successful people – Dad worked for an aviation company as an engineer, Mum was a lawyer. I was an only child, and everything was very proper. They were busy, and away a lot, and they made sure I had the best of everything. But what I didn't have was a lot of fun – I struggled to connect with other kids even then, I was just too used to being with adults and life being a serious affair.

'When they died . . . everything fell to pieces. I missed them desperately, and I suppose it made me even more isolated. There were a few other family members around, but they'd never been close. An uncle I'd never met who had no interest in taking on an adolescent boy. An aunt who I quite liked but who had four kids of her own and didn't think she could cope with another. Grandparents who were way too busy.

'So in the end, I came to Briarwood because, not to lay it on too thick, nobody else wanted me. That simple.'

Wow. He tells this story quietly and calmly, barely displaying any emotion at all – which is lucky, because I'm feeling enough bucket-loads of the stuff for both of us. My childhood was chaotic and not without its complications, but I never, ever felt like nobody wanted me. My mother was always loving, my siblings loved me enough to torment me every day, and I was always surrounded by mess and noise and energy.

I imagine Tom as a child, living first with parents

who didn't sound like a barrel-load of laughs and then in that dark little room at Briarwood, and it breaks my heart. It explains so much about him: his awkwardness around people, his preference for solitude, even the fact that he's so neat and tidy. He's basically never properly been a kid.

I think I'm still feeling a bit tired and emotional from my public display of crying in the café earlier, and don't want to plummet back into that particular black hole. This is his story, not mine, and I have no right to hijack his pain.

I lay one hand on his thigh, and give his leg a squeeze. He's staring off at Wurzel, eyes screwed up against the glare of the sun. I know how hard it probably is for him to talk about these things, and feel privileged that he's shared it with me.

'Well, sometimes people are just stupid,' I say, leaning into him. 'And it does help me understand why you're so fond of the House on the Hill. Now you'll bring it back to life.'

And maybe, I think silently, bring himself back to life with it. I vow that I will do my very best to help with that. I'll have him sliding down banisters and dancing to inappropriately cheerful pop music and splashing in that fountain and maybe even daring to leave a cup unwashed on the drainer.

He nods, and places his hand over mine, and we sit quietly for a few moments. It doesn't feel uncomfortable, this silence, but after a while, I start to wonder if the whole hand-holding, thigh-touching thing might be sending out mixed messages.

As soon as the thought crosses my mind, I tell myself off. It's an arrogant leap on my part to think that he'd even look at me that way. He could have seventeen gorgeous girlfriends back in London. Or be married. Or be gay. I really have no idea – and I'm sure I'm reading too much into it all. Basically because he's the first man I've met who's made me feel even a teensy bit interested for years.

'What about your life now?' I say, getting up and pouring out some more orange juice as a way to extricate myself from the touchy-feely stuff. 'Do you have . . . people? Friends? Girlfriends? Dog walking buddies? Online game partners? Clients, at least?'

He accepts his topped-up juice with a nod of thanks, and I deliberately take the chair opposite him instead of next to him. Little Miss Boundaries – that's me.

'Clients . . . well, the joy of being a mad inventor, once you reach a certain level at least, is that you get to lock yourself away in your attic and create without the need to talk to many people. I do have online game partners and people I chat with – but they're all called things like CheezWizz99 and Gandalf the Magenta. Girlfriends . . . not really, no.'

I raise my eyebrows, and smile. This sounds intriguing, and he looks a bit embarrassed and uncomfortable.

'What does "not really" mean?' I ask, not letting him off the hook.

'It means . . . well. I know a few women. The building where I live, it's not exactly your normal tower block. It's more a really expensive dockside development that also has a swimming pool and a gym.'

'Ah yes. I've heard that you city slickers are keen on such things. So that's how you manage to stay all . . . buff . . . without doing Iron Man contests or rowing along the Thames? No insult intended – but you are in good nick for a bloke who claims to spend his whole life locked in a darkened room tinkering with a soldering iron.'

He glances down at his own body – long, strong, packing out that *Star Wars* T-shirt very nicely thank you – and makes a fake surprised face. As though in his own head, he's just a weedy little geek boy, and he has no idea how this physique happened at all.

'I suppose. I like the gym. I like exercise. I like doing things where you can set goals, and count reps, and push yourself . . .'

'I bet you have some magic techno gadget that allows you to track it all as well, don't you? Something brilliant you invented all by yourself?'

'Well, it's called a FitBit, Willow – and sadly I didn't invent it. But yeah. I have one of those. And this gym . . . it's the social hub for the building, you know? It's mainly young professional types, people working in London from other countries, quite a high turnover. And that's where—'

'You meet all the hot women who find your winning

127

combination of eccentric charm and killer biceps completely irresistible?'

He grins, and looks so irresistible that I understand why.

'Kind of. It doesn't happen that often. And even if they do like the look of the killer biceps, the eccentric charm soon wears off after a couple of nights. Funnily enough, most women don't actually enjoy lying in bed planning out how to defend the block against the zombie apocalypse . . .'

'What? They don't know what they're missing! But . . . well. I don't know what to say really. Would "I'm glad you're getting some" be appropriate?'

'Totally appropriate. What about you?'

I realise as he asks this – inevitably, I suppose – that we are veering dangerously into that territory that men and women sometimes venture into when they're interested in each other. The human being version of dogs sniffing each other's bits, trying to find out if there's another mate on the scene. The little dance we do before we try and stick our tongues down someone's throat in a nightclub. Not that I've ever done such a thing, of course.

'Lord, no,' I respond quickly, wanting to nip it in the bud. 'I don't have time for anything like that. When I was younger, yes – there were some romantic moments that usually involved insane amounts of Scrumpy and committing arrest-worthy acts on the beach. But not now. All of that's behind me.'

'Behind you? And you're what . . . not even thirty?'

'Technically, I'm not. But my years are a bit like dog years, you know? For every one I spend on the planet physically, I think I age by seven. I'm not complaining about it – everyone has their shit to deal with – but there just isn't the time or space for anything but coping with work, life, and . . .'

'Your mum,' he supplies, quietly.

'Yes. My mum. But don't start feeling sorry for me – she's worth it. And a lot of the time it's not that bad at all. I know it's going to get worse, and the unpredictability is a major bummer, but we get by. Long term, all I get told is that nobody really knows what will happen next . . . but for as long as I can, I'm going to be here for her, and keep her life as steady and stable and enjoyable as I can. Whatever happens, she's still my mum. She's worth missing out on disastrous first dates and Tinder for. And I'm lucky, I have a lot of really great friends.'

'I noticed that. You are lucky. But you know what you mentioned earlier, about your brothers and sister? What about them? Can't they help out? Not that I'd suggest you're missing much with Tinder or whatever, but wouldn't life be easier if you had your family around?'

Girls Aloud have moved on to 'Something Kinda Ooooh', which is one of their silliest and finest songs. It is totally inappropriate as a background to this conversation, and I wish I was singing about their toot-toots instead.

'It's complicated,' I reply, kicking my boots against each other as I talk.

'I have an IQ of a hundred and forty-eight. I can cope.'

'Ha! Show off . . . and it's not complicated like a quadratic equation. It's complicated like . . . okay, we have different dads, for a start. Angel, Van and Auburn have one father, I have another. They, along with my mum and their dad, all lived together in a commune in Cornwall. Yeah, exactly – a commune! I suspect there were a lot of lentils. Anyway, their dad died, when Angel was only quite small, like four or something. Then mum got pregnant with me, and as soon as that happened, they all left.'

'Who was your dad, then?'

'I have no idea,' I reply, honestly. 'I'm not altogether sure she knows either. Reading between the lines, relationships weren't exactly traditional there, and according to what she's said since and what she's written in her memory book, she went through a bit of a tough time after their dad died. Maybe she was looking for consolation, and ended up with a baby. For many years, for some reason, I convinced myself that my dad was Kevin Bacon . . .'

'That would be weird. But cool.'

'I know, right? I think I'd watched *Tremors* one too many times . . . but anyhow. Once I was born, she moved the whole family here. From what I can piece together, the kids didn't want to leave the commune – it's where they'd always lived, and suddenly they lost the one bit of continuity they had. Maybe that's why I was just never as close to them as they were to each other. I always wondered if perhaps they blamed me for making everything change.'

'You don't really think that, do you? You weren't even born!'

'I know. But families are weird. Feelings are sometimes pretty messed up things, aren't they? Not exactly logical – especially in this house, where logic was among the least prized of traits. Then as they grew up, I think Mum ended up being a victim of her own success. She always encouraged us all to be free-spirited, follow our hearts, find our own path in life . . . and she was genuinely thrilled when they all started doing that. Except Angel – she was always a bit broken-hearted about that name change thing.'

Tom nods, turning it all over in his mind. For a man raised in solitude it must all sound ridiculously complex.

'So they followed their own paths – all the way off into the sunset – and you stayed here. Do they know? About the Alzheimer's, I mean?'

'Angel does. He's only in Aberdeen, so I did tell him. He visited once, but . . . well, he couldn't hack it. She was having an especially bad day, and it was all too much for him. He was never very robust, our Angel. Too celestial for his own good. And the others? Well I genuinely don't know where they are, and neither does he. We get occasional postcards, or a nose flute through the post, but neither of them seems to have stayed in one place for that long. I couldn't tell them even if I wanted to.'

'That's not very convincing, Willow. Not in this day and age, and with names like theirs . . .' he replies, gently. Damn him and his superpowers.

'I know,' I say lamely. 'I've not tried very hard. I suppose

I got my hopes up that Angel might come back and play big brother, and when he ran away as fast as his Volvo could take him, it was horrible. I was so disappointed, so I decided not to put myself in that position again. You know – a position where I'm . . . vulnerable.'

'Hey,' he says, smiling, and reaching out to take my fingers from my mouth. I didn't even notice, but I was apparently chewing my fingernails. Darn it – there goes that expensive Shellac manicure I never had. 'I get that. I've spent my whole life preferring to be on my own rather than risk being vulnerable. It's not a crime. And you're strong, you're doing a brilliant job. I admire you, and everything you're doing – but maybe it's time? As you say, things are unpredictable, but they're only going to head in one direction.'

I stare at my kneecaps, which I suddenly find fascinating. He's entirely possibly correct. And deep down, I understand that they have a right to know. Mum might have pushed them off on their journeys to self-enlightenment, and they might choose to stay on the road. But is it really up to me to make that decision for them?

I don't reply, and he doesn't push the issue. I think we've both had enough soul-searching for one day – or possibly for a whole lifetime.

'Come on,' says Tom, standing up. He grabs hold of both my hands, and pulls me to my feet. 'It's "Love Machine". I bloody love this one . . . let's dance like nobody's watching . . .'

Chapter 11

I don't see Tom for a few days after that, which is possibly not an altogether terrible thing. I talked more to him about my family situation that afternoon than I have for years, and it left me feeling raw and exposed, like a live wire dangling in a monsoon.

Not that he did anything to make me feel like that. In fact, he swept me away in a good half-hour boogying session that left us both sweaty and laughing. For a hermit, he has some moves; I suspect he's practised along to all those disco scenes in *Guardians of the Galaxy*.

He even stayed for dinner which was, as promised, provided by Cherie. That's a good thing – I can cook, but it's sometimes a battle with my mum. She loves cooking and is never happier than when stirring a big pot of something wholesome, messing with herbs from the garden, or baking.

The problem is that these days, the process confuses her. Following recipes is almost impossible, and even dishes she's been making for decades can go bad. It's one of the ways her condition makes itself most obviously known, apart from the memory thing – doing set actions in a set order can slip beyond her grasp. Not always, and not with everything, but the cooking? It can be a nightmare.

Many times, she's insisted, and I've ended up sitting through an awful meal while we both pretend to enjoy it. No fun at all.

That night we had butterbean and rosemary soup from the café, with thick wedges of chunky bread that Laura sent round to us. It was all very pleasant. Mum was a little on the hyper side, after a whole day of being a superhero, and I wasn't sure how she'd react to someone new being in the cottage. She might accept it as normal, or she might attack him with a frying pan while accusing him of breaking in to steal her kids.

In the end, something even weirder happened – she remembered who he was. And not in a putting-the-pieces-together-and-coming-up-with-flange-bracket kind of way, but in a real way.

One of the mysteries of her memory is the way it's all spooled up inside her brain, looped around and tangled, so weird bits pop out at strange times. She might struggle for days to remember the word for 'those woollen things you put on to keep your legs warm' – tights – but then tell a brilliant story in glorious technicolour about something that happened three decades ago, with all the skill of a seasoned after-dinner speaker.

She took one look at Tom, who was outside playing

with Rick, and walked right up to him, still wearing her cape and red knickers. She paused in front of him, hands on hips, and gave him a thorough eyeballing. For a moment I feared a bout of the gut-wrenchingly cringe-worthy behaviour that she occasionally displays, where she thinks she's a lot younger than she is – but his virtue was safe.

Tom handled the situation perfectly. He stood up straight, made eye contact, and said very simply: 'Hi there. My name is Tom. It's nice to meet you.'

'I know who you are!' she replied, suddenly all smiles. 'I wasn't sure at first, but now I'm up close I know who you are . . . you're Tom, the boy from Briarwood. You wouldn't leave your room, would you? Just locked yourself in there with all your gadgets. Mrs F was worried you were going to burn the place down.'

'Yeah . . . there was a small incident with a waste-paper bin, once . . .' he answers, looking sheepish.

'There was. That's right. A bin and a chemistry kit. Terrible smell for ages afterwards. I used to bring you books, didn't I? About all the inventors. I tried to get you to join the workshops, but you were having none of it. Didn't like the look of the other wild lost boys. Goodness, how nice it is to see you. It seems like it was yesterday, doesn't it? It does to me anyway – but as you probably know, I'm a little bit . . .'

She pulled a 'ga-ga' face and formed the traditional 'screw loose' gesture at the side of her head with her fingers, while also making cuckoo noises. I had to laugh. Every now and then, you get one of these brilliant moments of clarity and self-awareness, where she's able to poke fun at the whole situation.

'It doesn't seem so long ago to me, either,' Tom said, sitting down with her to reminisce about the good old days. If, of course, you could describe the time when you moved to a children's home after your parents had died and the rest of your family had rejected you as 'the good old days'.

He went back to London for some business the morning after, and life settled back into a less disrupted routine. I took Mum to the hospital in town for one of her check-up days, where she meets with her doctors and occupational therapists and a counsellor and does some memory work.

It's always hard, and this time was especially tough. When she's surrounded by people she doesn't really know, she can look so bewildered it makes me want to cry.

She's always had a lot of dignity, my mum – she can even stand on her head and look dignified – but something about a day at the clinic seems to suck it all out of her. She starts bravely, but after a day of tests, and answering questions, and feeling like she's somehow failed it all, she deflates from the inside out.

She clings onto me, getting smaller by the minute, and asks repeatedly – in a hushed whisper to hide her embarrassment and confusion – 'Where are we? Who are these people? Why are we here?'

Everyone there is very kind and very understanding –

sadly, they've seen it all before – but it always drains me as much as her, seeing her distressed and unsure of herself. I always make sure I'm at home with her the next day, as it can leave her unsettled for a while. We try and write it all down as we go, for both our sakes, and go over it when she's feeling calmer.

Today is her first time back at the day centre, and she seemed happy and eager to go. I left her with Carole this morning, clutching her notepad and waving me off as I tootled down the drive in my van. For all I know, she immediately turned back to Carole and asked who the hell I was, but at least she was smiling. Sometimes I have to take what I can get – even if I suspect she's faking it.

Now I'm here, back at Briarwood, and I've had a lovely day. I've been scrubbing and polishing and whistling away, Bella by my side. We've been a regular grime-fighting team, out here in the wilderness, singing along to a collection of Disney tunes. Belting out the words to 'A Whole New World' is very life-affirming, I can tell you.

Pleasantly tired, I'm having my lunch break sitting on the rim of the fountain in the sunshine, watching the insects buzzing around and the birds dive-bombing, feeling thoroughly alive and thoroughly affirmed. I've filled in my own notepad, even doing a few terrible sketches of the building, and I'm enjoying the solitude. Nothing quite makes you appreciate solitude like spending a day in a busy hospital.

I'm about to pack up and leave for the café when Tom

arrives – bizarrely wearing a smart suit. Rick Grimes gallops over to lick Bella, and I give Tom a little wave as he walks towards us, emerging from the dense green trees in the clearing. The sun dapples through the leaves, dancing on his shoulders, and given my recent Disney binge I think he looks decidedly prince-like.

'You look pretty,' I say, gesturing at him and his fancy outfit. 'Have you just won second prize in a beauty contest?'

'Yes, I collected ten pounds and everything . . .'

He perches next to me on the fountain, and looks around at the lush wilderness of the gardens. The sun is zinging off the windows of the house, and it looks a lot less haunted just for that. I see him already planning and scheming as he takes in the building, and wonder if that brain of his is ever quiet.

'You look warm,' I say. 'Peanut?'

He accepts both the oddness of the words, and the offer of peanuts, throwing one up in the air and catching it masterfully in his mouth.

'I am warm,' he says, tugging off his jacket and opening a couple more buttons on his white shirt. 'Had to actually go to a proper meeting for once. Not about work – about this place. I'm considering hooking up with some colleges and apprenticeship schemes, and thought I'd better look more like a successful designer than a serial killer hermit who lives on his own in a caravan in the woods.'

'Oh. Cool. How did it go?' I ask. 'And can I please have permission to stroke your head?'

He stares at me, and I see the lopsided grin creep across his face as the amusement sets in.

'You are completely random today, Ms Longville. Even more than usual, I mean. The meeting went well – lots of good ideas and possibilities. And yes, you have permission to stroke my head.'

I reach up and run my fingers over the closely shaved hair. It's dark, and soft, and actually pretty thick even though it's so short. It feels exactly like I thought it would.

'Thank you,' I say, laughing at myself. 'The first day I saw you – as a grown-up – I wondered if it felt all velvety, like a mole's bottom. I'm glad to report that it does.'

'Wow. I don't think I've ever been compared to a mole's arse before, but . . . thank you? I have to keep it short or I look insane – it just grows up and out like a big fuzzy halo, and makes me look like I spend all day playing video games and smoking dope. How are you, anyway? I was hoping I'd bump into you . . .'

I'm still trying to imagine him smoking dope – and failing – when I realise I haven't answered him.

He's right. I am especially random today. It happens when I've had an intense few days with my mum – the sheer relief of being on my own makes my mind expand rapidly from its protective, curled-up ball, grasping in wonder wherever it goes. It reminds me of one of those school science experiments where you drop some food colouring into oil, and it blobs all over the place like a lava lamp.

'All good, thanks,' I say, screwing the lid of my flask back on. 'But I'm due at the café in half an hour. Hi ho, hi ho, it's off to work we go! Maybe we can catch up tomorrow?'

He nods, and looks slightly worried, as though he has something to say that he's nervous about. Maybe my scrubbing hasn't been quite up to standard. Maybe he doesn't like my dwarf singing . . . no. My dwarf singing is perfect, it can't be that.

'Spit it out,' I say, nudging him so hard he almost falls backwards into the empty fountain. 'I can tell something's buzzing around in your mole arse.'

'Yeah, it is,' he replies, smiling as though he's been caught out. 'Two things, actually. One of them is the café – I've had a text from Cherie, who seems to have used her contacts at NASA to get hold of my number, telling me I have to start coming for ballroom dancing lessons. Is that an actual thing, or have I accidentally wandered into an alternative universe?'

'Ah. Right. Well, probably both. It's Edie's birthday soon – you know, Edie of the House May? And she'll be ninety-two years old. Cherie's thinking, which you can't dispute, is that once you reach that age, every birthday is a landmark. So there'll be a party, and Cherie and Laura like planning parties – I think they get some kind of sick thrill from making the rest of us play along. We've had horror shows, country and western nights, Mexican siestas, the lot . . . and this time it's *Strictly*-themed. Edie's nuts for

Strictly, so we're all learning some basic ballroom to make her night special. This is mandatory. If you refuse, Cherie will make your life a living hell.'

'I'm pretty sure that being forced to have ballroom dancing lessons with a bunch of people I barely know *is* my idea of a living hell, but okay . . . will you be there? And how will you manage a quickstep in Doc Martens?'

'I'm more of a Charleston girl, I think. And I have a wide and varied collection of Doc Martens, some of which are very glittery and perfect for such an occasion, thank you very much. Don't diss the Docs. I never saw Fred Astaire in Converse either, pal.'

He raises his feet and shows off the shoes he's wearing today – proper, grown-up ones, made from soft, shiny black leather. They look like they cost a lot of money, and go perfectly with his posh suit. Neither of them, though, go perfectly with him, and I prefer the goofy tops and jeans.

'Fair enough, twinkle toes,' I reply, after he wriggles them around proudly. 'So that's sorted. You will endure Cherie's torments for the sake of Edie. I know you haven't met Edie yet, but believe me, when you do you'll be happy to undergo any variety of tortures just to make her smile. So what was the other thing you wanted to talk to me about?'

He nods, and looks more serious. He gazes off at Rick and Bella, and seems to be weighing up whether to speak or not. His nerves are making *me* nervous, and I fidget next to him as he builds up to the big reveal, whatever the hell it is.

'Okay. Well, this is a bit more complicated,' he says eventually, turning to face me. 'And I hope you don't mind. I haven't done anything with this information – that's entirely up to you. But . . . well. I've found your brother and sister.'

Chapter 12

The lunch shift at the café is insanely busy, which is exactly what I need. It feels like half the world's population has decided this would be the perfect day to go fossil hunting in the spring sunshine, and they all need feeding and watering.

The day is warm, but with a nip in the breeze as it whips up from the sea, so people often wander into the café looking a little chilly, hands shoved in pockets and hair blown wild. The big hit of the day is smoked salmon fillet with spring greens, which thrills Laura as it's her new seasonal dish. We also serve approximately 7,000 tuna melts, 3,798 bowls of pea and sorrel soup, 1,508 rhubarb toffee muffins and precisely 4.2 million assorted chocolate bar milkshakes.

By half two, the kitchen is wrecked. It should have crime scene tape around it, and sinister-looking men in hazmat suits wandering in and out wearing gas masks. It's crammed with plates that need putting in the dishwasher, denuded lettuce heads, squeezed oranges, empty cartons for recycling, and the discarded foil wrappers of all the Kit Kats and Twixes and Turkish Delights that Laura used during the Great Milkshake Rush of 2018.

When it all finally tails off and we get the chance to breathe, the only people left are myself, Laura, Cherie, Laura's sister Becca, and both Edies.

Little Edie is sitting on Big Edie's lap over in the bookshelf corner, contentedly cooing away and trying to pull off her namesake's glasses. Big Edie is reading out loud to the baby – it's a racy scene from Jilly Cooper's *Riders*, but I don't suppose it'll do any harm.

'Do you think Little Edie will grow up with a liking for fit-looking men in jodhpurs now?' I ask, gesturing towards the pair.

'Who doesn't have a liking for fit-looking men in jodhpurs?' replies Becca, sipping her coffee and looking at me as though I'm mad. Fair point. Behind her, Cherie and Laura have formed a very small human chain, passing plates and mugs towards the dishwasher while singing along to 'Stairway to Heaven'.

It's usually at this stage in the proceedings that we'd all sit down, eat something delicious, and talk about absolutely bugger all. But today, I need to keep busy, and stop my mind from wandering over the same territory again and again – because it's Groundhog Day on Planet Willow.

I take myself outside with a bin bag and a cloth, stylish yellow rubber gloves up to my elbows, and get busy clearing the garden tables. Laura introduced kids' lunchboxes this week, and it feels harsh to crush up all the brightly coloured little cardboard dinosaurs and princesses and pirates. Harsh but possibly cathartic, and I work my way around the whole place swooping them off tables and up from the grass, scrunching as I go.

When I've done that, I even venture into the doggie crèche field, and do a poo collection. This is a job most of us try to avoid, for obvious reasons, often waiting until there is a handy teenager around to wrangle into it. Bella trots around at my ankles, tail wagging, laughing at me, I think. Ha ha, she's saying, you humans and your silly ways – we own you all!

I deposit the deposits in the depository, and finally let myself stand still. I feel about as enticing as what I've just scooped up, and am blatantly trying to stave off the moment when I have to make some decisions. Or at least think about making some decisions. Perhaps pencil in a provisional date to have a meeting with a sub-committee to compile an action plan to provide a framework for developing a strategy about possibly making some decisions.

'Oh, shit . . .' I say out loud, kicking the bin, full of exactly that, in frustration.

Predictably enough, the bin topples over and I spend the next fifteen minutes picking up small black bags full of canine excrement. I now need to scrub myself all over, and maybe pay some extra attention to the inside crevices of my brain. I peel off the gloves, and lob them into my bin bag. I'll treat myself to a new pair, maybe something from the latest Stella McCartney Domestique line.

I sit down on one of the benches and stare out at the sea. I take some deep breaths in and out, and let myself relax as I watch the waves crashing over the sand. I can hear the sounds of children squealing and dogs barking and the jingle-jangle tune of the ice-cream van arriving in the car park.

I remind myself that the world is not coming to an end. People are still buying 99s with flakes; dogs are still chasing sticks; kids are still paddling in water cold enough to make them yell with delight. The Earth is still revolving around the sun, I am still sitting here, breathing slowly, surviving. I have grass beneath my feet and I am solid – I will not float away like an unloved helium balloon.

I have no idea why I feel so stressed and tense. Stress I'm used to – in fact it's like caffeine, and I use it to get through the day. But the tension is something different. All the various bits of my poor body feel clenched and pinched; even my toes seem to be scrunched up in my boots.

Well, it's not a complete mystery, if I'm honest. It's because Tom has found my brother and sister. This is not a big deal, I know. It's not as though they've been missing for twenty years, and he's discovered them being used as alien slave labour in the outer reaches of the solar system.

They haven't been missing – they've been living the life my mum always wanted them to live. The life she